BO
The Bound Series

Bound by You

Enemies - Lovers Romance

C.L.MCGINLAY

bound by you

BOUND SERIES BOOK 2

CHARLOTTE MCGINLAY

Copyright © 2024 by Charlotte McGinlay

Bound by You – Bound Series Book 2

Second Edition

All rights reserved. No part of this publication may be reproduced, distributed, or transmitted in any form or by any means, including photocopying, recording, or other electronic or mechanical methods, without the prior written permission of the publisher, except in the case of brief quotations embodied in critical reviews and certain other non-commercial uses permitted by copyright law.

This book is a work of fiction. All names, characters, locations, and incidents are products of the authors' imaginations. Any resemblance to actual persons, things, living or dead, locales, or events is entirely coincidental.

contents

Trigger Warning 1
Prologue 2
Chapter 1 21
Chapter 2 35
Chapter 3 46
Chapter 4 54
Chapter 5 63
Chapter 6 76
Chapter 7 86
Chapter 8 94
Chapter 9 105
Chapter 10 112
Chapter 11 124
Chapter 12 136
Chapter 13 145
Chapter 14 155
Chapter 15 162
Chapter 16 173
Chapter 17 183
Chapter 18 194
Chapter 19 210
Chapter 20 215
Chapter 21 224
Chapter 22 233
Chapter 23 238
Chapter 24 246
Chapter 25 259
Chapter 26 267
Chapter 27 277
Chapter 28 284

Chapter 29 291
Chapter 30 301
Dear Reader 308
About the Author 309
Other Books by Charlotte 310

trigger warning

This book contains depictions of graphic sexual situations, cheating between the H/h, violence, and child trafficking. If any of these things offend you, please do not read.

prologue

Phoebe – 19 Years Old

I'M SITTING on my bed, reviewing my studies for my Animals and Society class. I have my headphones in, and I'm bobbing my head to Bon Jovi, when something, or more like someone, flicks me on my forehead, making me jump up and scream. Looking into my sister's laughing eyes, I narrow mine at her and remove my headphones. She's lucky I wasn't armed.

"Seriously, Selene, you nearly gave me a heart attack!" I snap, causing her to laugh aloud, and I tilt my head. She hasn't laughed much in the past week. Things between her and Father have been extremely tense lately. I'm not sure why, because she and Father have always had a close bond; he has spoiled her rotten over the years, and it used to make me jealous half the time, especially when he can't stand to look at me. But I think it's because I have my mother's bright green eyes, while Selene has his brown.

Despite having white-blond hair down to my waist, hair the same color as his, I'm more of my mother's copy at 5'5" and slim, while Selene is a copy of him except for her hair, which is more of a sandy blond bob, nearly the light brown of mothers. Selene is 5'9" and curvy. She's three years older than me, but we'd been best friends for as long as I can remember…until I returned home three years ago.

When our mother was killed by the Romanians when I was only ten, it was Selene who comforted me despite mourning herself; my father refused to acknowledge me, and we've had an estranged relationship since. It was my grandmother, *Yia-Yia* Athena, whom I barely knew, who raised me, while my father took sole responsibility for my sister.

I had to move in with her at her cottage in Greece, because she wanted nothing to do with my father. She was a carbon copy of my mother, with light brown hair and bright green eyes, so the decision for my father was easy; he didn't want her around, either, and even for the few days she did stay here for my mother's funeral, it was tense. She died three years ago, and I had to return to our family home on Long Island to a father with cold eyes and no love or sympathy. He only shows love to my sister.

It's something I've struggled to forgive him for.

I don't feel welcome here. I spend most of my time either with Sergi, my best friend, and my pseudo brother, or in my room, which is at the back of the house instead of the one I had growing up that was a few doors down from his and Mama's. If I see my father around the house, I slink back into the background to make myself invisible, which isn't hard to do when I was shy and quiet before he sent me away. I filled that role again with ease; no one knew my other side.

My sister being in my room now is a rare thing. We're not as close as we once were.

"What are you doing?" Selene asks, shaking me out of my head.

I push her away.

"My schoolwork," I answer, rolling my eyes.

"Boring, you don't need to do schoolwork; it's not like *Bampás* would let you do anything anyway. It's all for show to make him look good in front of his business partners and alliances. You'll be married off." My heart stops. She's said this time and time again; it's like she wants to hurt me. I ignore her every time because I don't want to believe it, especially when my father is adamant that she works for the family, despite her being engaged.

I have always wanted to be a vet; animals call to me more than humans. I look to my windowsill and see my black and white cat, Ares, sunning himself. He's only three years old, and he's the last thing my *yia-yia* gave me before she passed away in her sleep. My father wanted to shoot him, but I threatened to run away if he hurt him.

It's the first time I stood up to him, and it's also the first time he has ever slapped me. It took everything in me not to hit him back or grab the knife that I always have inside my boot to stab him. At the time, Sergi was here to pick me up and, thankfully, intervened. For the first four months after my return, Sergi took Ares for me, until he convinced my father to let me keep him.

"I know, but I can still try!" I whisper, playing my shy self while looking at my cat. My sister hums, making my stomach sour. I love my sister dearly, but she changed a lot over the years I was gone. She doesn't think before she speaks; she was my best friend before I left, but she's now really self-centered. She loves living life with maids and butlers, not doing anything for herself, knowing her father wanted her to get a degree to work at one of our restaurants, despite not giving me the same option.

She'll do several courses at NYU twice yearly to placate him. Now, though, she's saying she likes women instead of men, and hoping to get more attention from him. She's attention-hungry and greedy and, besides Sergi, she was the only other friend I'd ever had. Sergi has told me time and time again that she can't be trusted, and I know it's true, which is why I keep my "shy" persona up around her, and watch her. It's safer for me that way.

Selene drags me out of my thoughts when she grabs my pillow, hitting me with it. I look at her in shock, and she laughs. I quickly get into action, grab the other one, and hit her with it, pretending we're young girls again. She squeals, and we end up in a pillow fight just like we used to as children, ending it in a fit of laughter that dies quickly with a throat clearing. We look up, and the smile on my face disappears as my father, standing at 6 feet in a tailored black suit, stares at us like he doesn't recognize us. I quickly look down at my hands, not knowing what to say. He never comes to my room, and we haven't said two words to each other since he slapped me at sixteen.

"I need you both in my office in ten minutes. Make yourselves presentable." Selene nods with a smirk, then goes to Father, and kisses his cheek, before running to her room to get ready without saying a word.

I look up and state, "Yes, *Kai*," and bow my head a little.

He frowns a little; his eyes flash with guilt, but he quickly hides it behind his mask, and they turn cold again. He nods and turns to walk away while I stand in the same position, looking at my hands. He turns a little, his brows furrowing at me once more, and then he leaves.

A tear slips out of my eye, and I quickly wipe it away. We've gone from a loving family to one daughter treating him like he walks on water and the other treating him like the second-in-command to the Greek Mafia Godfather of the Night—*Nonos tis Nychtas*—that he is, resenting him for all that he's done and for what I had to endure. I hurry to my bathroom to get ready.

Maybe one day my dreams will come true. I will become a veterinarian, and my father will love me again—but a dream is all that is.

Alexandr – 26 Years Old

This fucking sucks!

I love my life.

I love all the pussy I can get without the need to hide mistresses. Well, that was until my father decided I needed to help the family like Damian did. I can't exactly say no when, technically, it should have been me married to Sofia and becoming the next Pahkan and Italian Don next year and not him. But with my ADHD diagnosis at five years old, it's just not possible, and—I wouldn't admit this to anyone, but I'm glad I don't have that responsibility. I played on my diagnosis a lot to ensure I didn't take over. I just feel guilty that Damian was pushed into it instead, and is now struggling.

His wife, Sofia, left him on their wedding night. He loved her fiercely but was in denial about it. They've been best friends since he was twelve, after her father and ours pushed him into it. Instead of the usual alliance where the bride knows there's an arrangement, he's had to ensure she falls in love with him without her ever knowing the truth. He was in the rebellious stage, where he'd deny his feelings and fuck around with sluts who didn't care he was taken, then feel fucking guilty for straying on the woman he loves. Unfortunately, she found out, then left after marrying him, leaving her phone with two incriminating videos on it.

Sofia may have seemed quiet, but she was fierce and refused to be like her mother, who turned to alcohol and sleeping with her husband's men after he started ignoring her and having mistresses left and right. Damian has struggled for the past two years; he's been drowning, and he's looking for her, as we all are, but as a punishment to her, he's also trying to move on.

His dick has other ideas, though, and he just doesn't know how to stop trying. I worry it'll be too late by the time he realizes his mistakes, and when he finds her, his guilt will eat him alive. Because he *will* find her. My heart hurts for them. Sofia is like a sister to me. I love her dearly, and the guilt ate me alive, knowing what our families and my brother had done to her. She felt betrayed, and decided to take the easy way out, disappearing without a trace. And I love Damian. He's my blood brother, my best friend, but he's also a fucking idiot. He needs to get his head out of his ass fast.

This leads me to where I am now, on Long Island, staring at the fucking *Kai*, or second-in-command of the *Nonos tis Nychtas'* mansion. I sigh, shaking my head.

I stand to every inch of my six-foot-three-inches and square my shoulders, running my hands down the sides of my short dark hair, and ensuring the long hair on top is still slicked back.

I knock on the door and a butler answers. He takes me through the dreary house; it's like a shrine to his deceased wife, who was tortured, raped, and killed by the Romanians, which turned out to be his brother's fault. He helped them get to her as a fuck you to his brother for taking the woman he originally wanted but who was already pregnant with Selene. The brother doesn't know Basil is aware of his betrayal; it's taken him nine years to get his plans in order.

The butler takes us through the foyer, then right down the hallway, coming to a stop by a black door. He knocks, and then enters with me behind him.

Basil Adino sits behind his black desk, leaning back in his chair, his white-blond hair in in disarray. He looks stressed, but that's expected. He's been planning and plotting a takeover for nearly a year.

Between the Bratva, the Italian Mafia, and Basil's men, whom he has recruited behind his brother's back over the years, the takeover should go smoothly, and the revenge will be bittersweet. Normally, other Mafia wouldn't get involved with these types of situations; it's between family, despite how close my father and Basil are, but Adrian is rumored to be dabbling in human trafficking and, we may be assholes, but we stop at flesh-peddling.

"Alexandr, please come in and take a seat." He sighs. I tilt my head and take a seat in the comfy-looking black armchair. "Is everything okay, Basil?" I question. I'm concerned about him; he's alright for a Greek. He and my father are close friends, and they have been since infancy. They grew up together, much to Adrian's dislike. Adrian has tried to start a war several times over the years, but Basil always quashes it.

"Sorry, Alexandr, just worried for my daughter Phoebe is all."

I nod. I'm aware of the youngest Adino child who was forced to move to Greece with her grandmother. Sergi was upset when she left. Those two are really close, like brother and sister, really. I haven't physically met her, though. He'd meet up with her once a month, and they'd talk on the phone, but he always ensured to keep her away from us.

Adrian had taken a liking to her after he had her mother killed when she was ten. He had an auction site set up with several takers, including the Romanians. Basil did the only thing he could think of and sent her away. He didn't have the manpower to take his brother on, and the only way to get her to leave was to make sure she thought it was because he didn't want her anymore.

Apparently, she's the spitting image of her mother except for her white-blond hair, so it was easy to convince everyone he couldn't stand being around her when he just wanted to keep her safe. He struggled with the decision and spoke to my father at length about it. He loves his daughters but had to do what was best at the time. When his mother-in-law passed away in her sleep, he had no choice but to bring Phoebe back. He's kept her at arm's length, though, for her safety, but keeping up the façade eats him alive every day.

He sighs deeply. "The marriage contract cannot be with Selene, my eldest."

I raise my eyebrows at that. Don't get me wrong, I don't want this marriage at all, but I also know I must marry an Adino for us to help take down his brother and the trafficking enterprise in our area. Otherwise, it would start a war.

"What's changed your mind?" I ask in a calm voice, not looking forward to explaining this to my father. He will think I did something to fuck things up and, for once, I didn't.

"I haven't changed my mind; I just changed the bride," he states solemnly, and I furrow my brows in confusion.

"Despite it being a marriage in name only, for appearance's sake, it needs to look real for Adrian to not get suspicious, and he will not believe it with you and Selene." He looks pissed, and I keep quiet, waiting for an explanation. "She was aware of the rules; she signed the documents but decided to make a sense at a family gathering—more for attention than anything. Selene states that she is in love with some college student."

I arch a brow. "Okay…? Why can't we kill the guy? She's clearly breaking the written contract we both signed and wants to get back at me for not giving her my black card," I state.

His answer shocks me.

"*She*. It turns out my daughter is not into men anymore and thought it best to bring the young lady to our family restaurant while Adrian was there." He runs his hand through his hair, frustrated. "She also has a new passion, painting, and the classes she's chosen cost $15,000 for three months." I try not to fucking laugh. Selene is one of those people who tries new things just so she doesn't lose a life of luxury. She's very materialistic and spoiled. Basil is the kind of man who prefers the women in his family to take responsibility and earn their keep, meaning college. Degrees and jobs, which Selene does not want.

I've heard whispers of Phoebe wanting to be a vet and already in college taking courses, according to my fuck buddy, Mindy. Selene's very jealous and has been planting shit in her sister's ear about their father not wanting her to work because she'll be married off, not that I gave a shit. Mindy likes to try and cuddle and have pillow talk after our fuck sessions, and Selene's whole "I'm into women" thing is definitely not true. Does she like eating pussy? Yes, she does. Mindy is her go-to pussy, but only when she knows I'll be there, too, which I'm certain her father knows nothing about.

I've only ever fucked her mouth and ass, never her pussy, and usually I watch as she gets tongue fucked as I fuck the women in between us, much to her dismay. Still, I think this is a ploy she didn't think her father would take seriously. Too bad she made it too public...but this is perfect for me. I never wanted to marry Selene; her personality is shitty. That's why I've bitched nonstop over this arrangement. I know I would have killed her within a few months.

She's basically only good for her asshole and mouth. The last time we met, as per the contract rules, we didn't have a chaperone. She tried to make a show of ownership after a barista flirted with me, then pushed the crocodile tears when I told her to knock it off. So, the fact she's now into the opposite sex is hilarious, and I don't have to marry anyone.

He must have noticed my expression because he lets out a little chuckle.

"Don't get your hopes up, Al. Like I said, I'm switching brides, which your father has agreed to, too. I just wanted the opportunity to tell you, and for you to meet your new bride today." He smirks at me, and my stomach bottoms out.

Shit, fucking Dad. I wait patiently for him to announce which of the women in his family will be my new bride.

"Phoebe."

That is all he says, and I stand up fast.

Fuck no, she's just a kid.

He puts his hand up and states, "She's nineteen. You're only seven years older than her, and I think this is a better way to keep her safe until our plan comes to fruition next year." He says it so calmly, but I can see the fury in his eyes. He doesn't want her to marry me just as much as I don't want to marry her. Selene fucked things up; she knew her sister would have to take her place, but she put herself first anyway, out of jealousy and greed, like she always does.

Well, this is going to truly fucking piss her off, but she should have known better.

Just as I'm about to open my mouth and tell him there's no fucking way I can marry his youngest and that we'll figure something else out, there's a knock on the door.

"Enter," Basil commands in a cold voice. I look at him with a raised brow, and he shakes his head a little. I tip my chin to him before moving over to the wall. The door opens, and Selene walks in, her hair curled in a short bob. She's wearing a black maxi dress that dips too low, with a pair of sandal wedges that stick out as she walks. She's added a few inches to her 5'9". She has caked her face with makeup, and I shake my head wondering how the hell I ever thought she was beautiful.

Every time I've seen her, she looks like a fucking clown.

She sees me, stops, and smirks, licking her lips, obviously thinking the meeting is about our arrangement and hoping for an apology and my Black Amex. I shake my head. What the actual fuck? She cannot be this thick, can she?

"Selene, get out of the doorway and sit down," Basil booms from his desk, clearly pissed at how she's dressed, his face red from her actions. She startles and starts to move forward, and just as I'm about to ream her fucking ass for the shit she's causing, all because she's a whiny, spoiled brat, my voice stalls in my throat, and I swallow my tongue at the vision before me in the doorway.

Standing at maybe 5'5", with a body men dream of—slim but with just the right curves around her waist and hips. Long white-blond hair cascades down the back, minimal makeup, and she's wearing a simple, light pink t-shirt, jeans that hug her so nicely that her ass looks edible, and a pair of pink and yellow DCs.

This is Phoebe Adino, and she's looking stunning without even trying. Well, now I understand why Sergi kept her away from us. She's a fucking vision.

She has her hands in front of her, linked together, and she's keeping her head down. She goes to the chair I vacated, and sits down, not once looking up from her lap. Selene looks at me, and then at her. I want to roll my eyes.

What does Selene expect? She told her father she's a lesbian so, even if he doesn't believe her, she's made the family—including Adrian—aware of her preferences.

Basil clears his throat as I lean against the wall, crossing one leg over the other while wrapping my arms over my chest, staring at Phoebe, and waiting for the shitshow.

Fuck, she's beautiful.

"Selene, as you have publicly announced you are in a relationship and have met the woman of your dreams, the marriage contract you signed is now null and void." I look toward Selene as she pales, and I want to chuckle but hold it in. I look back at Phoebe, and she hasn't moved from her position. I can feel myself already getting restless, but I try to tamp it down. I forgot to take my medication this morning. Shit, my heart races the longer I look at her. That's because of my missed meds, right?

Basil continues, "Because of this, we have canceled your arrangement with Alexandr."

Selene sits forward. "But Father□—"

He doesn't let her finish, raising his hand to silence her. She frowns and narrows her eyes but listens.

"An arranged marriage is still going to take place, but instead of you, it'll be your sister who will marry Alexandr Volkov." I notice Phoebe tense, but she doesn't say anything. Selene looks in her sister's direction and sneers at her, and I shake my head. *She's* the one who caused this with her lies, and yet she looks at her sister like she's at fault.

"The wedding will take place when Phoebe turns twenty-one, but the conditions are still as follows: Alexandr Volkov and Phoebe Adino are to meet as required, one day a week, chaperoned by a guard. The marriage is of convenience; therefore, love is not required. Once the contract is signed, the husband will not father any children with another woman. A child must be conceived within one year of marriage. Public displays of affection with others are prohibited. The wife-to-be is to attend every gala, all parties, and business dinners with her husband-to-be. After five years of marriage, if both parties agree, a divorce may be obtained.

"This marriage will be the anchor to an alliance between the Greek Mafia and Russian Bratva. You are to follow these rules. Do you understand Phoebe? You are now bound by Alexandr."

At each rule stated, Selene relaxes a bit more, until her father talks about the divorce. At that, she tenses again, realizing that not only do I have to stay married to her sister for five years, but Phoebe and I could also decide to stay married and, if I'm being honest, like hell will I let her divorce me.

She's fucking mine. My heart races at the thought of losing her. What the fuck? I barely know her.

Where in the fuck are these thoughts coming from?

I shake my head at my confusing thoughts. Phoebe tenses at each rule; she doesn't want this, but she hasn't got a choice. She can thank her sister for that, and so should I.

Fuck, she's mesmerizing.

Finally, she speaks for the first time, and her voice is sweet and soft. My heart aches at her words, though, and by the looks of Basil, his is torn in half.

"Yes, *Kai*."

She stands, bowing her head a little, then gives her sister a nod. Selene frowns back, narrowing her eyes, obviously pissed that Phoebe didn't fight it. Without looking at me or making eye contact with her father, Phoebe goes for the door.

With her hand is on the handle, she freezes at the sound of my voice.

"Phoebe, Friday afternoons at the Precious café on Fifth Street at 3 PM—we will meet. Understand?" My voice is void of any emotion despite my heart racing. I'll make her fall for me because I won't let her go. She half turns her head and nods, then leaves without so much as a huff.

Selene is just about to open her mouth when her father dismisses her with a wave. She glares at him, but he ignores her, and she stomps out of the office, slamming the door. I shake my head and look back at Basil when he speaks again.

"We'll have to keep an eye on Phoebe. I think she'll run. She may seem quiet and shy, but she's changed some since living in Greece. She hasn't managed to hide it as well as she thinks; we'll have to triple security."

I nod. Why argue if you can try to disappear? It makes sense as to why she didn't make a fuss.

But she's not going anywhere. There is one rule *I will* be breaking, because there will be no divorce. I'm never letting her go.

I smirk.

one

Phoebe – 21 Years Old – Two Years Later

I sit in the precious café with my student books out in front of me, the biochemistry course kicking my ass today.

This paper is worth 70% of my grade.

I don't have classes today, but I had to get here at 6 AM, much to my disappointment. I like my sleep.

I huff, feeling grouchy.

"What are you huffing about, *malen'kaya ptitsa*?"

And I cannot stop the grin from forming on my face. Alexandr stands over me, his bright blue eyes looking at me like I'm all he sees. He's in a suit this morning, a black shirt underneath his suit jacket with a couple of buttons undone, showing some of his muscled chest and his ink, making him look amazing as always. I breathe in and smell his musky cologne and something that is just him, then smile wider.

"You're late, *agapi mou*," I say, smiling, and he chuckles. He bends down and kisses my forehead, making my heart flutter. Then he places a peck on my lips, and he grins back at me. We're meeting much earlier than our usual 3 PM date, because of his niece's birthday party and a meeting he couldn't get out of. Alexandr's sister-in-law did invite me, but I have too much coursework to complete before tomorrow. I made sure to buy little Mila the biggest princess treehouse I could find, which Damian found hilarious when she screamed at me.

"I love you, Phe Phe; you're my favorite."

Sergi and Damian scowled hard at me, while I was in a fit of giggles with Sofia, trying to hold each other up. We'd become very close when she came home, getting along right away, like long-lost friends, much to Sergi's disappointment. Apparently, I'm his, which brought Alex into the argument, stating that I'm engaged to him, so technically, I'm his. They argued for an hour over it.

Alex's mom, Maria, and dad, Dimitri, tried to hold in their laughter when Mila stated I was the favorite, which didn't last long when Mila turned to her uncles, saying, "You have some catching up to do."

She said it so seriously that Sofia and I fell to the floor with tears running down our cheeks. His parents lost it then, too, while Damian was biting his lip, eyes full of amusement, and Sergi chased after her. She giggled like crazy while Alex came to us and helped us up.

"That's it, the wedding is off. I can't have my fiancée take my niece from me, too. It's bad enough, fighting with Sergi for the top spot," Alex stated, *dramatically. We were back on the floor, dying of laughter. After that, he just shook his head at me.*

I smile at the memory. I love his family. After I finally decided to give the idiot a chance, we became close. Maria is like a mother to me, and Dimitri, well, he's more of a father than my own, and Damian says I'm the little sister he never wanted, which makes me smile every time. Family—that's what we are.

I finally feel like I belong.

"Are you ever going to tell me what that means, sweetheart?" Alex questions, bringing me back to now, and I chuckle.

"I told you, learn Greek."

He shakes his head. This is our weekly argument. Once he finally learns Greek, he'll know that I'm in love with him. It's something I didn't think could happen. The first meeting we had, I sat here with my books, like I am now, but ignored him while he tried to talk to me. I'd done that for two months, when he finally had enough and placed a very delicious aero mint muffin in front of my nose.

I looked at it, then at him, then back at the muffin, and stated, "Okay, we can be friends." Then I proceeded to eat said muffin while he chuckled. Since then, we have become extremely close; he was my first kiss, and I don't regret it. He's my everything.

He speaks, pulling me out of my thoughts again. "And how many times have I told you I haven't got the patience to try and learn it, even when I remember to take my meds?" He tears off a part of one of my muffins and shoves it in his mouth, and I shake my head at him. He's lucky I love him; otherwise, he'd lose a finger for taking my muffins.

"Then you'll never know. Stop using your ADHD as an excuse to not have to learn something. We both know you can concentrate better than anyone actually knows." I smirk, and he scowls at me, hating when I give it to him straight. "Did you finally win, favorite Uncle? You know, it seems as though I'm her favorite aunt and all," I tease.

His brother's wife left him on their wedding night after she found out he was cheating on her with other women, and that their whole relationship was a lie. She wasn't aware it was an arrangement like mine and Alex's, so she was hurt and betrayed, and decided to run. Something I contemplated several times in the first few months, but suddenly, there were extra guards, so I had no hope. I tried twice, but Alex and my father just shook their heads at me and continued with their days, like the guards didn't drag me back to the house.

Alex sighs, and I put my pen down, join my hands over the books, and tilt my head at him, giving him my full attention. He mirrors my body, doing the same.

"No, I swear, when this boy is born, Sergi isn't getting within an inch toward of him, and neither are you." He looks down, sulking, and I place my hands over his on the table, squeezing them to placate him, letting out a little chuckle.

"I'll tell you what I told Sergi yesterday; she loves you both the same, just not as much as me, so stop sulking." He looks back at me and smiles, chuckling, and I grin.

I love his smile.

We stay at the café for a couple of hours while he tries to help me with my class, but we laugh most of the time instead. It's like this every time.

He drives me home in his Mercedes-Benz like he does every time we meet, drops me off at the front door, kisses my cheek, then pecks my lips after giving me a tight hug. Then he waits until I'm inside before driving away.

I sigh. He's the highlight of my days.

I walk into the kitchen, where my father and sister are sitting at the kitchen island laughing quietly, and as soon as I enter, they stop. I ignore them both and head to the fridge for a water bottle. My father doesn't even acknowledge me, while my sister, the only person other than Sergi I thought I could count on for years before I was sent away, sneers at me. It's been this way since it was decided I would marry Alex instead, but she was hiding her disdain for me long before that. I'm just not sure why.

To her, I'm no longer her sister, but a man-stealing whore—her words, not mine, even though she's the one who decided to play games to get her own way. I ignore her and walk out again, heading to my room to continue my schoolwork. Despite having to marry, Alex is very encouraging about my studies and my dream to become a vet. He's even looked up some veterinary schools in the area. I smile, feeling lucky to have him and his family's support.

Walking up the stairs, I hear my sister snark, "I don't understand why she's still living here, *Bampás*. I asked you to move her into her own apartment; why can't you? You know I made a mistake with Alexandr, and now I have to watch my sister steal my man, my future."

I pause on the staircase, tears forming in my eyes while I hold my breath, waiting for his reply, hoping he doesn't disappoint me.

"I already told you, *pepõn*, she's already tried to run twice, and now that I am *Nonos*, I need to keep her close before the wedding in five months. Once she's married off, we don't need to see her again, okay? Then, after five years, Alex should divorce her, and if you still want him, go for him. I doubt she'll care."

I don't wait for her reply and run to my room. Once inside, I lock the door, then turn and slide down until I'm sitting on the floor. My eyes tear up, but I hold them in.

Since being with Alex, my "other side" has slipped away. I used to be immune to their cruel words, but now it's starting to get to me. The tears fall, and I curse myself, willing my training to kick in. I take a deep breath, wipe away the traitorous tears, and stop feeling sorry for myself for the lack of family I have inside this house.

I grab my school stuff, place them on the bed, and go to my bathroom, quickly scrubbing my face to hide the evidence the tears left behind, before putting my mask of indifference back on, and go to finish my homework like the last twenty minutes did not happen.

About three hours later, my phone pings with an incoming message. I look at the time, and it's just gone lunchtime. I furrow my brows and put my schoolwork away, then grab my phone. I know it can't be Alex; he said he had a business meeting before Mila's party, and Sofia will be busy with Maria getting ready. Sergi is on "Mila duty", while Damian will probably be hovering around Sofia. She's heavily pregnant with their second child, and he's apparently turned into a helicopter—her words, not mine...unless she's messaged me to tell me she killed him and needs help hiding the body. I chuckle and pick up my phone. My smile disappears, and my brows furrow in confusion.

Unknown: link attached.

I place my thumb over it. I know you shouldn't click on links that someone you don't know has sent you, but I'm a curious person. I click on it, and I turn up my volume when I hear someone talking. Suddenly, I'm regretting clicking on the link.

"It's about time you got your sexy ass here, Selene," an unknown voice states.

I don't know who the woman is, but she's tall and blond, wearing only lacy, black lingerie. I scowl, confused as to why someone sent me this. I already know Selene dabbles with the opposite sex; it's not news to me. She'd go to anyone willing to spend money on her.

"Sorry, Daddy took me shopping because he wouldn't send my sister to her own apartment. Still, she stole my fiancé, the least she could have done was fuck off."

I sigh, realizing exactly how much of a spoiled bitch she's become over the years.

"Don't worry, darling, it's only for five years, but speaking of Alexandr," the unknown woman smirks, walks over to my sister, and kisses her. I gag and go to end the stream but the unknown woman speaks again, making my heart drop to my stomach.

"He's finally knocked me up, so we can all be a happy family once we get rid of your sister. We just have to let the marriage paperwork go through so he can get the inheritance you mentioned, and then you contact your guy for the Romanians to pick her up. Alexandr has agreed." She laughs, and I can't believe it—Alex wouldn't sleep with these women, especially not with my sister! This must be a setup, and he certainly wouldn't give me to the same men who killed my mother.

I wait for Selene to laugh like it's a joke, but she doesn't, she just smiles wide, and I shake my head. How can she hate me so much? She blames me for something I had no control over. My father gave me the arranged marriage because she's the one who spitefully let everyone know she was seeing a woman.

It takes a moment, but something hits me…what she just said…. How the fuck does she know about my inheritance?

I wait to see if they say anything else, but they don't. They start to make out, making me want to throw up, but then I hear a click of a door, and they both pull apart at the sound of a male voice, a voice that I have come to love. The man who bound me to him speaks and comes into view, unbuttoning his black shirt, the same one he was wearing this morning, his six-pack coming into view, with his ink showing over his left chest and shoulder, and I shake my head in disbelief.

"You both started without me?" Alex smirks as I start to sob heavily. I turn my phone off just as he grabs hold of Selene and shoves his tongue down her throat, and bile rises in mine. I run to the bathroom just in time to spew up everything I have eaten. I feel like someone is pulling my insides out. I guess *this* was his important meeting.

Now I know how Sofia felt. How the fuck did she take her husband back?

I wash my face and quickly brush my teeth, and I look up at myself in the mirror, my hair a mess and my eyes are still shining with unshed tears. I take a deep breath. My body wants to fall apart, but my mind is taking over; my training finally kicking in. My father doesn't want me, my sister is a selfish bitch, and now my arranged fiancé is not only sleeping with said sister but has also gotten another woman pregnant. My blood runs cold, the mask I've perfected around my so-called family cracks and falls away, and I push my heartbreak aside as my stone-cold bitch persona resurfaces.

Time to complete my plan. The contract is now void!

I go to my closet and find the duffel bag I've had packed for a few years, and open it. All my essentials are still in there, as are my weapons and a debit card with over a hundred million dollars that my *yia-yia* left me in her estate and savings. Thankfully, it's under a ghost account, that can't be traced. My father and sister were pissed when they realized they got nothing in her will; I just didn't know they were aware of what she left me—my inheritance.

I take my phone out, open my emails, and send the feed from the link that I saved on my phone to Damian so he can see why I have left. I type CONTRACT VOID in the subject bar. I know he won't see this for at least three weeks; Sofia is close to her due date. I debate sending her and Sergi a message, but I shake my head because they'll contact Alex.

Going to my balcony, I throw the bag over the side of the second-story mansion that has been on my mother's side of the family for generations. I heard my father promise it to my sister last year, which is laughable because once my mother passed, it automatically went into my grandmother's name. I'm aware my father tried to appeal but didn't get anywhere; he signed a contract stating he would have no legal right over the property.

It's now in my name.

Maybe I should send them an eviction notice—fuck, that would be funny.

After looking around to make sure it's clear and no guards are about, I climb down the trellis connected to the wall, and once at the bottom, I look around again. Security on me has been lax over the last year, so I'm guessing I was no longer classified as a runaway despite what my father said to Selene this morning. When I notice it's clear, I pick up my bag and make a run for it across the massive green lawn, and once I get near the gray wall with stones sticking out of it, I look around again. I see a guard heading my way and quickly jump into the bush to my left, but as I lean against the wall for support, something slices down my arm, and I have to hold in a scream of surprise, clamping my hand across my mouth. I can feel the blood dripping down my fingertips. I look down and see a large open wound on the left side of my arm. It's sliced open wide and will most likely need stitches.

Shit.

I look at the wall and notice sharp blades sticking out of it, and I roll my eyes. Of course, the uneven stones have blades attached.

The guard walks past without stopping as I hold my breath and wait five minutes for him to enter the guard house. Once he's gone, I quickly open my bag, grab the medical kit I put in there, and grab some butterfly strips. I place several on the wound as tears leak from my eyes, and I try to stay quiet, biting my lip hard, then wrap my arm with some gauze. I look around again, see it's clear, and get back to the wall to climb over. I notice the blades are all on the left side of the brick, so I know to keep my feet and hands to the right side. I quickly climb up, and as I reach the top, I chuck my bag over, and promptly jump six feet down.

I land on my ankle funny, and I curse inwardly, rolling my eyes. So much for my training fully kicking in. I gently jog on it to the Buick I had hidden here, in a deeply wooded area, a year ago as a precaution.

My ankle and arm hurt, but nothing is going to stop me. As I get to the car, my heart races, and I keep thinking someone will jump out and shout, "Ha!" I look around again, and the coast is clear. Quickly, I shove my bag in the trunk. I climb into the driver's seat, start her up, and drive off without looking back. California is a good place to settle, even if it is a 43-hour drive. I have looked it up more times than I can count since being forced back to the US.

I've already planned my stops on the way, starting with Cleveland, then Chicago, Iowa, Denver, Utah, and Las Vegas, finishing in Mendocino, where I'll be continuing my veterinary studies at the University of Redwood. I've had an open spot there since graduating high school, and I'll be staying in the ranch I bought two years ago with my inheritance, in my grandmother's birth name; Athena Angelos. I smile a sad smile.

I may be bound by Alexandr, but I'll make sure I still live life as freely as I can.

two

Alexandr – 28 Years Old

I WALK into the hotel room where I'm meeting Selene and Mindy. Fuck, I'm horny after spending some time with my girl.

I know I shouldn't be doing this, especially with Phoebe's sister, but a guy has needs, and once we're married, I won't sleep with another woman again. I love Phoebe, I do. I've fallen for her hard, but I don't want to pressure her. I know she's a virgin, so I'll just get my fix from other women until then. I only have to wait five months until she is fully mine anyway, and as long as she never finds out, we'll be fine because, like fuck am I going to go through what Damian did.

As I walk in, they're both already making out, and I smirk.

"Both starting without me?" They turn to me with big smiles, and I unbutton my black shirt, drawing it open. I grab the back of Selene's neck and shove my tongue down her throat while thinking of Phoebe. She moans loudly, her hands going to my chest, gliding up and over my large shoulders as she shoves my shirt off. She drags her sharp nails down my chest, making me growl and groan.

I rip my mouth away from hers and smirk at her whimper. Mindy walks between us and drags her tongue from my nipple down my torso, and her hands go to my belt, quickly undoing it, then pulling my jeans and boxers down my legs as pre-cum starts to dribble out of my dick. I grab my hard cock from the base and squeeze it as I move my hand up, creating more cum at my tip. Selene licks her lips and gets on her knees.

She licks the cum from my tip, and then sucks my cock into her wet, warm mouth. I groan, grabbing Mindy by her neck, and shove my tongue down her throat. I'm not always keen on Mindy; she's territorial, whiny, and tries to trap men. She's done that twice to me, but she's a good fuck, so I go back once or twice a month, but always ensure she swallows my cum. I don't come in her pussy anymore, despite being in the doctor's office with her when she gets the shot.

I'm pulled out of my thoughts as Mindy bites my bottom lip and sucks it into her mouth, then starts to kiss down my neck, gently sucking it while Selene deep-throats me. Her right-hand glides up my leg to my heavy ball sack and squeezes gently before pulling on them, while her left goes to Mindy's soaking panties, pulling them down before she glides her hand up Mindy's left leg, then uses her fingers to circle Mindy's wet cunt before shoving two inside her. We can hear the gushing sounds each time she moves her fingers in and out, and that's all it takes as I unload my cum into Selene's waiting mouth. Her makeup runs down her face as I push my cock as far as it will go, keeping it there, causing her to gag, but she swallows it all like a good girl.

I remove myself and go grab a beer from the mini bar, removing my pants completely in the process. Mindy lays on her back as Selene lays on top of her, spitting in her mouth, sharing my cum with her.

Fuck, that's hot.

My dick perks up again, the greedy bastard, as Selene starts to tongue-fuck Mindy, her fingers twisting her nipples, leaving Mindy to moan and thrash under her. I take a swig of the beer as I watch the show.

Mindy's legs are wide open, her juicy pussy dripping all over the floor, and Selene rubs her cunt on Mindy's. I grab hold of my cock again and stroke it as hardens for a second time. More cum drips from my tip, and I put my drink down and get behind Selene. I bend down, placing my face right where their pussies are rubbing together. I get right in there and lick Mindy from her ass to her cunt, catching Selene's at the same time. Both women moan, so I do it again and again and again, until they're both squirming and moaning. Selene comes first, screaming out her orgasm as I lick the dripping fluid.

Mindy goes next, and I drink it all up.

I lean back, and Selene gets off Mindy and lays down next to her, both heaving heavy breaths from their orgasms.

I go over Mindy's body and lay on top of her, placing my hard cock at her entrance and thrusting hard into her, and she screams out before moaning as I bend down, taking a pebbled nipple into my mouth while my right hand goes to Selene's pussy, and I thrust two fingers into her. My left-hand grabs hold of Mindy's left leg, and I lift it over my shoulder as I fuck her hard and fast. As Selene is about to come, I remove my fingers from her, causing her to whimper, and shove them in Mindy's mouth. She sucks them as I remove myself from her heat.

I yank my fingers from her mouth, and she whimpers, too. Before I get onto my knees and grab hold of Mindy's hips and turn her onto her stomach, I look at Selene and state, "Get that juicy cunt under her mouth, Selene." She obliges instantly, causing me to smirk, and once she is in place, I grab Mindy's hair and use it to move her mouth to Selene's cunt.

She goes willingly and starts to feast on it like it's her last meal—fucking sluts, the both of them. I take the tip of my cock and place it at the entrance of Mindy's ass. I slowly push in, passing the tight ring of muscles, and she moans and groans. Once I'm all the way in, I pause to give her a minute, and once she wiggles her plump ass, I pull out, then shoot forward hard. The room is filled with our moans and grunts. Selene goes off first, her hand gripping Mindy's head as she rubs her pussy on her face, coming hard.

Mindy's next, screaming her orgasm as I press my finger on her clit rough and hard, just the way she likes it, and just before I come, I quickly pull out and grab Selene by the back of her neck and shove my cock into her mouth, and come down her throat. Her hands grip my ass cheeks, digging her nails in and swallowing it all, not caring that I just had it in Mindy's ass.

I groan out my orgasm. Once I know I'm done, I pull out and smirk, then go to grab my clothes, making both women pout. Selene is pouting more than Mindy, but they know the score.

"You're leaving already? I wanted you to fuck my ass next," Selene whines, and I just chuckle.

"I've got my niece's birthday party; I'm late as it is. Enjoy yourselves for a bit and send me videos, will ya?" I chuckle again, sending a wink, making them both smile wide. Once dressed, I give them a one-finger salute and leave, their moans following me as they start making out again. I go to the hotel room permanently booked under my name, quickly shower our little sex fest off, and change into some new clothes. I'm wearing me black, Henley V-neck shirt and dark blue jeans, and I arrange my dark, messy hair, ensuring the short sides are slicked back. Once I'm ready, I leave, heading to my car in the garage.

As I get to my car, I check my phone and chuckle.

> Damian: where the fuck are you? Your niece wants one of her favorite uncles to hurry his ass up; she's not happy that her Auntie Phe-Phe won't be here.

I chuckle. I may pout, but I love how much that little girl loves Phoebe.

I reply.

> Me: I'll be there in 20. Tell Sergi to not take her in the pool until I'm there, or I'll kick his ass.

He replies instantly.

> Damian: too late; should have been here earlier. No violence at Mila's party. Sofia's orders!

Fucking Sergi. I shake my head. I don't mind, really; it's just fun and games for us both. Finding out Sofia had a child without any of us around was heartbreaking. We're just trying to make up for lost time, and God knows how Damian feels about it all, even though it was all our fault that we weren't involved.

As I get into my Mercedes, my mind drifts back to Phoebe and how she'd feel if she found out about what I've just done and have been doing for two years. Shaking my head, I put my car into gear and head to my brother's to celebrate my niece's birthday, two months after her actual birthday. Phoebe won't ever find out about what I've been doing; I've filmed most of our interactions, so if Selene decides to stir shit, then her father will have proof of what his oldest is doing in her spare time.

It takes me about half an hour to get to my brother's, and I smirk. Damian is about to be pissed, and I'm pretty sure when Phoebe finds out what I got our niece, she'll be jealous. She keeps saying Ares needs a playmate.

I shake my head, grab the pet carrier and the box that I picked up on the way here, and go through the house to the garden.

I grin as Mila screams, "*Dyadya* Al."

I quickly place the carrier and box on the table near Damian, who raises both eyebrows at me, wondering what I've bought her now. He was pissed about the pony I got her eight months ago, so this should be fun. I love riling him up. I just smirked and caught my niece, who's got a hood towel on and some sauce around her mouth.

"Hey, my *malen'kaya*, are you having a good time?"

She nods, then looks over to her gift when she hears a *meow*. I chuckle as Damian sighs. I look toward Sofia, and she has the biggest grin. Damian notices, and he scowls at us both. I try to hold in my chuckle while Sofia laughs outright; she knew what I was getting Mila, and so did Sergi.

Mila screams, "A kitty," and we all grin at her.

"What do you want to name her?" I ask as Damian helps her get the tabby kitten out of the carrier.

"Star," she states, and I get emotional, causing Damian to chuckle at my expense. I just shake my head.

I kiss her on the head as my mother comes over and kisses my cheek, smiling from ear to ear, then helps Mila take her kitten and all its belongings inside. I kiss Sofia on the cheek, and she smiles at me as Mila comes back out, running over to me. I catch her, lifting her high, making her giggle, before she gives me a big kiss.

"Thank you, *Dyadya* Al," she whispers, and I hold her tight for a few minutes. We hear a splash, and I roll my eyes at Sergi's attempt to get her to remember he's here, but she hears him and wiggles to get down, then proceeds to jump into the pool and Sergi's waiting arms. I narrow my eyes at him, and he narrows his back. We have a standoff for a few seconds, and then we chuckle while Sofia shakes her head. As I'm about to ask how my nephew is cooking, my phone rings, and I furrow my brow.

"It's Basil; I'll be back in a minute." Sofia frowns, knowing he would contact her husband if it were business, so she knows something must be up with Phoebe, but nods her head, knowing I need to answer the call.

"Basil, what can I do for you? Is Phoebe okay?" I say as I walk over to the side of the garden, away from the others. He knows about the party today; he was invited but could not make it. He had meetings with the Irish mob, so I know this must be important.

"No, she's not okay; she's fucking gone. I have video evidence of her climbing down her trellis and off into the fucking woods over the wall. She's run."

My heart stops.

"What do you mean she fucking ran? She was perfectly fine when we met this morning," I snap down the line, causing a few people to look at me, concerned. Damian catches my eye, his brows furrowed, but I shake my head at him. He doesn't need this stress on top of being a husband, father, and a fucking Pahkan and Don.

Basil sighs. "I don't know; all her things are still in her room. She only had one duffle bag on her back. She's left her phone, and when we checked where she hid in the bushes away from the guards, there was a trail of blood. Apparently, she managed to cut herself on the bladed wall." He sounds broken, but I can't think about that right now. My fiancée has fucking left me. She made me fall for her, and she fucking left.

A thought comes to mind.

"She doesn't have money; you ensured she only had a limited amount on her card, and it's a card we can track, right?"

He clears his throat and sighs again.

"She has an inheritance of over a hundred million from my deceased wife's mother. She left everything to Phoebe in an untraceable account that none of my men can find. The only person who knows where the money is, is Phoebe.

Selene tried to get close to Phoebe again when she returned because she wanted the money. She heard a conversation between me and the lawyer when I tried to block Phoebe from accessing it, but it didn't work. Athena's will was airtight. She also owns this house; everything her grandmother owned was put in her name. Phoebe isn't aware that I know all this, though."

I look toward the pool and notice Sergi throwing Mila into the air, and I scowl. That's where I should be right now, pretending to fight with my brother from another mother over who's the favorite uncle—but instead, my heart is being torn into pieces.

"How the fuck are we supposed to find someone on the run with that amount of money? Why the fuck did she run?" I say loudly, my anger getting the better of me. We were fine this morning; what the fuck happened between then and now?

Selene and Mindy quickly come to mind, but I squash that thought; there's no way she knows about that or the others.

"I don't know, Alexandr, but I intend to find out. The Romanians still want her; someone else put her up for sale last week. We're trying to figure out who. All I know is they weren't working for my brother. We must find her before they do."

I growl and am about to comment when suddenly, I hear a cry and turn around to see Sofia leaning over while my brother looks at her in horror.

"Shit, I've got to go; keep me updated." And I hang up without saying anything else; he'll be pissed but will cool down when he realizes why.

I'm fairly sure Sophia's gone into labor. Fuck!

three

Phoebe – Five Months Later – Current day

I WALK OUT of class with the biggest smile and an A plus on my animal disease paper. I thought I flunked it. Yesterday was supposed to be my wedding day, and I struggled all day, my heart missing what could have been.

A month after I left, I found out that the woman in the video, Mindy, was bullshitting, but it still doesn't change the fact that he was fucking her, and he'd been sleeping with my sister, too. I've been trying to move on and move forward, and it's behind me now. I've done well to keep my mask in place, and I will continue to do so because I'm learning to live my life for myself now, not my so-called family and a man who decided to destroy everything we had. Now, I can actually celebrate tonight with friends that *I* made. I grin stupidly to myself; there are only five and a half more years until I get my dream.

"What are you grinning about, Missy?" Abby, my roommate and friend, questions me as she approaches me with a large caramel latte.

Yes! I could kiss her.

In fact, I do. I land a big, old, sloppy one on her cheek and say, "Thank you. I've been dying for this all day." She laughs out loud, shaking her head at my antics. I hold my result sheet and say, "Guess who aced the test." She squeals and hugs me, nearly knocking my drink out of her hand, causing me to growl and giggle simultaneously, making her laugh louder. Then I take my drink before she almost drops it.

"We have to celebrate tonight!" she states, and I nod. I wasn't too sure about her at first, especially with what happened with my sister. I figured out that she was using me for our grandmother's money. I just wish I'd realized sooner, but I won't make that mistake again. Abby, though, is different. She's loud and proud, and she gives no shit to anyone, with her hair dyed in rainbow colors. She's curvy, with dark brown eyes, just an inch taller than me, and the best person I know.

"I was thinking we hit up Kevin's in town."

She nods, and I chuckle. She has a crush on the bartender, James.

She scowls at me. "He will notice me today. I'm going to wear the skimpy, black dress that just covers my ass, and my dark red heels. He'll be eating out of my hand, you watch."

I shake my head at her before I notice Brent, the guy who keeps trying to ask me out, out the corner of my eye, and I quickly link my arm through Abby's, pulling her toward the parking lot.

She hasn't noticed him, which is good, because the last time he approached me, she turned crazy and started threatening him, and as much as I'd have liked to see her kick his ass, I have a persona to keep.

We head to my Buick, which's still going strong, and go home. We carpool every day because we share most classes together. She wants to become a veterinary nurse, while I want to become a vet, so it's perfect.

The ranch I bought under my grandmother's name is amazing. I have yet to buy any animals, but I will once my course load lightens. The ranch house itself is one story. It's a white building with red trim around it, and a white wraparound porch.

It has an open-plan living room and kitchen, three bedrooms, and two and a half baths. The two main bedrooms have a full bath attached, and the third one has a shower and toilet across the way from it. That room I gave to Ares, well, he took it, more like. It's technically a guest bedroom that he stole, but I don't mind. He's five years old now and very chunky, and he loves it.

After I moved here and went to register for classes, I bumped into Abby in the office. She was screaming at the administrator about how her roommate was into orgies and offered for her to join in. I felt bad and offered her a room at my ranch. She nearly toppled us to the ground when she rushed and hugged me. She's been working her way into my life since. I even helped her decorate her room in pink and green. It already had a queen-sized bed, a walk-in closet that was just a little bit smaller than mine, and a dresser. We went to Target and got her some green sheets and artwork for her walls. Then we sat down and went over the bills and groceries that we decided to cut in half, because the ranch was fully paid off.

As I pull up to the house twenty minutes later, I lose it in laughter, making Abby look at me like I have lost the plot. I quickly put the car in park, grab my phone, and get my camera app up, hitting record. Abby is still looking at me, not noticing what I have seen until she turns her head, and both her hands come up and cover her mouth.

"Oh my God," she states before bursting out in laughter.

Currently lying on the ground, wiggling around, is my friend/kind of boyfriend Oliver, who is trying to kick the goose from the farm across the road away from his ass, as it has a good grip on it with his beak.

He looks up, notices us, and scowls at the tears running down my face.

"Are you seriously sitting in your car recording this? Fucking help me, babe," he shouts, and I lose it again while Abby clutches my arm, struggling to talk through her laughter.

"F-fuck, t-this is the funniest s-shit I have e-ever seen."

I nod in agreement.

"Babe, please!" he bellows, and I pass my phone to Abby and head out to help, all while still laughing.

"I'm glad you find this funny, babe, but remember, paybacks are a bitch." He sneers at me, and I start laughing hard again, making him roll his eyes before he screams out in pain as Goosy, the goose, bites down harder. I quickly but quietly walk up behind him and catch him by the neck. I don't have a net, so this method will have to do. I pull the bird close to my body. I reach down and wrap my arm around his body, holding the wings in place, and grasping both legs with one finger between them.

I gently pull up while Oliver quickly gets out of the way, and I try to hold back my laughter but fail, because he glares at me as Abby gets out of my car, still laughing.

I gently stroke my index finger against Goosy's neck and ask, "Are you okay, baby? Did that mean man hurt you?" I coo to the bird, and Abby loses it again while Oliver glares at me. I just smirk, then walk the bird over to my pond. He'll head back home when he's ready.

After I place him on the pond, I head indoors. As I walk in, I go stand next to Abby to see what she's laughing at now, and end up using her as support, not able to hide the sheer amusement of Oliver using my frozen peas on his bare ass. He's pulled the back of his pants down while he ices himself. We end up on the floor, tears running down our faces, and he scowls again.

"Alright, laugh it up, and here I was, being the nice guy I am, coming to see my girl and ask about her test results, and this is the thanks I get: a bird attacking me, biting my ass, and you two recording it." He shakes his head at us, and we lose it again.

He pulls his pants back up and places his hands on his hips, glaring at us, and I chuckle a little before calming down and walking over to him. He softens, opening his arms, wrapping me up in them, and I place my head on his chest and sigh in disappointment—no butterflies or tingly feelings.

We've been in limbo for about four months now. I met Ollie through Abby after a month of living together. He works with James at Kevin's despite having his parents' money. He's got the boy next door look with blond hair, blue eyes, and a swimmer's body. He's been incredibly sweet, kind, and patient with me. I mean, we've made out a couple of times, but we haven't gone further. I struggle every time he tries to get intimate. My mind drifts back to Alex, and I instantly feel like I'm cheating on him, which is fucking ridiculous because I know for a fact he's not living like a monk, which is why tonight is the night. I'm moving on with my life, and I think I can be happy with Oliver, so I've decided to give him my virginity. I just need my body to play ball.

"Fancy coming to celebrate with us at Kevin's tonight? Seems as though I got an A plus," I ask as I look up at him, and he grins widely before he lifts me up and spins me in a circle.

"I fucking knew you could do it, baby; I never doubted you." I grin back. "Okay, baby, I'm going to head out. I'll shower and change, and be back in an hour and a half to get you girls, deal?" I nod as he bends down and places his lips on mine. They're soft and warm. He licks the seam of my mouth, and I grant access, his tongue tangling with mine. He slows the kiss, then pecks my lips again before heading out, and I sigh out loud.

"Still no spark, huh?"

I groan, banging my head on my kitchen counter. Abby chuckles softly and rubs my back.

"Are you sure you want to lose your V-card with him tonight, Phoeb?" she asks gently, and I lift my head to look at her, glaring.

"Yes. I think once we get there, the spark should be there, too, right? I need to try. I cannot keep moping for someone who doesn't give a crap about me. We'll use lube if we have to," I state, and she gives me a sad smile, then drags me to my room, where Ares has made himself comfy on my king-size bed. I walk over to him and pet him, making him purr, and I smile.

"Right, missy, leave the pussy alone and go shower. Wear your short, purple, lace dress, with your silver heels, your hair down in waves, and light makeup. We'll meet out front in 45 minutes," she commands, and I chuckle.

I stroke Ares and head to my double-en-suite bathroom to get ready. I shave everywhere, because tonight, I will finally lose my virginity, and Alex will not be in my mind. Right?

four

Alexandr – Current Day

I SMILE as I watch Mila swirl in her ballerina outfit as she practices her dance, ready for her show tonight. Maksim stirs in my arms, and I gently rock him, patting his butt while smiling again. He's the spitting image of Damian, and a happy little baby. At five months old, he's started to butt shuffle, and he always looks proud when he does it, too.

He settles as Mila curtseys, indicating the end of her dance, then bounces up and down, proud of herself, and I grin at her. I can't believe she's nearly four.

"How was that, *dyadya*? Do you think Phe-Phe will come to my show tonight?"

I give her a loving smile while rage builds in my gut. "You were perfect, *Malen'kaya*, but Phoebe won't be able to make it, sweetheart. She's still at college to learn to look after animals." She smiles a little and nods, and I sigh. She misses the woman she saw as a loving aunt when, really, she's a fucking selfish bitch. Mila gently leans over her brother to kiss my cheek, then heads to the kitchen to find her mama. Sofia is amazing with the kids, and Damian doesn't take it for granted to have her back in his life.

I look down at the beautiful boy in my arms, and I sigh. My mind wanders back to Phoebe as it normally does when I'm alone, and my thoughts are mine alone. Usually, I'd go out and do the grunt work for the Bratva; torturing is my specialty and helps me think of all the ways I'm going to punish her, but I can't when I have this little dude. I rub my finger along his cheek. I had never wanted to kill a woman before her, but she made me fall in love with her, then bolted without a word to anyone.

I shake my head.

I've been trying to find her, but not so we can pick up where we left off. No, I want to fucking punish the bitch for doing this. I never felt true emotions before, and now I feel like a fucking fool.

Sofia walks in, bringing me out of my head, and I smile at her. She smiles back and sits beside me, touching her son's head.

"How are you doing, Al?" she questions, and I lean over, kissing her cheek. She asks me every day, even though I wish she wouldn't, but I love her for it anyway. She's not just my sister-in-law, she's also my best friend, much to Damian's dismay.

"I'm fine, *Mladshaya Sestra*," I state, and she chuckles.

"You're a bad liar, Al, but I'll let you off today. Want to hear some good news?" I know she's struggling without her friend, too. I lean closer, hoping and praying it's something I can use on Damian.

"I'm pregnant."

My eyes widen in shock, and then I grin the biggest fucking grin. I wrap my arm around her shoulders and squeeze her tight, kissing the top of her head.

"That's fucking awesome, Sof. I'm fucking happy for you." She grins at me as Damian walks in; his face is angry, and I furrow my brows, but it changes as soon as he sees me with my arm wrapped around his wife. He grins.

"She told you about my magic sperm?"

Sofia rolls her eyes, and I chuckle.

"Absolutely no living with him now, Al," she states, then goes to take my nephew, and I pout, making her chuckle. "Come on, my boy, let's leave *dyadya* and your *papochka* to whatever man talk they're about to have," she coos at Maksim, taking him up the stairs, where Mila quickly follows with food. I chuckle again while my brother has a loving look on his face.

"What's up, baby brother? You looked pissed when you walked in," I state, and he clears his throat, taking a seat next to me.

"We're both fucking idiots when it comes to phones, aren't we big brother?" I furrow my brows, confused. What is he talking about?

"Have any luck finding Phoebe yet?" he asks out of nowhere, and I growl, not wanting to talk about the fucking bitch. According to Selene, she had already lost her virginity and was sleeping with two of her guards, and that's how she escaped. Basil and I have personally questioned and interrogated all of them, and none of them knew what we were asking about. We killed three who we thought were involved in her escape because no one is that fucking lucky, and when I do find her, she's going to fucking wish she'd never met me.

"No, both Basil and I have looked all across Europe because, according to Selene, that's where she would go. Greece is out of the question because it's the first place we'd look."

He nods and clasps his hands together while leaning his arms on his knees. He hangs his head a little before taking a deep breath, and I still. He only does this when he has something important to tell me that he knows I won't like, which explains why he didn't argue with Sofia taking the kids upstairs when he's just gotten in from the office.

"Spit it out, brother, we haven't got all day. Mila's show starts in a few hours, so tell me what you want, and we'll figure it out." He nods once and looks at me, his eyes assessing me.

"What did you do last night?" he questions, and my brows shoot up. That is not what I thought he was going to say.

"You mean the night that was supposed to start my honeymoon?" I say sarcastically, and he nods once. I tilt my head to the side, assessing him, and answer, "I had a threesome with two of the strippers at the club. Why?"

He looks at me and asks, "Have you had threesomes with anyone else or just the strippers?" I furrow my brows in confusion. Why the fuck is he asking me these questions? "Just humor me, please, brother."

I nod. "With Mindy and Selene, twice a month for years, why?"

He clears his throat. "Does anyone know about your meet-ups with them?"

I lift my brows now in surprise. "No, brother, just the three of us, and now you? Why? What's going on?" I'm getting agitated, and he swallows hard before sighing deeply.

"One of them has betrayed you, brother. Probably both of them were in on it together, I don't know. But you were betrayed."

I go to open my mouth to ask him what the fuck he means when he lifts his hand to silence me, and I grind my teeth. He knows I hate it when he does that shit.

He gets his phone out of his pocket.

"A few of our business associates have called the last couple of days, complaining about their emails going unanswered. When I spoke to them personally, they were still using my old email address, the one where I'd talk to women about our plans. As you know, I got rid of it out of respect for Sofia, but for some reason, my assistant didn't realize she never discontinued the account or sent out my new email address to some people.

I personally went through all the old emails myself, when I came across one from five months ago." He takes a deep breath; the look in his eyes tells me I'm about to explode, and I brace myself.

"It was from Phoebe."

My breath stops, and a lump forms in my throat.

"She sent me a live link she'd saved, and in the subject box, she wrote, 'contract void.'" He looks at me like I'm an active bomb in my hands, and I feel like I am one. Once I finally find my voice, I ask coldly, "What was the link?"

He unlocks his phone, goes onto his emails, and finds the one from my girl, and he clicks on it. When voices ring out a rage like no other consumes me.

"It's about time you got your sexy ass here, Selene," Mindy states, coming into view on the camera in black lingerie.

"Sorry, Daddy took me shopping because he send my sister to her own apartment. Still, she stole my fiancé; the least she could have done was fuck off." Selene gloats like the spoiled bitch she is. My body starts to vibrate with rage when Mindy speaks again.

"He's finally knocked me up, so we can all be a happy family once we get rid of your sister. We just have to let the marriage paperwork go through so he can get the inheritance you mentioned, and then you contact your guy for the Romanians to pick her up. Alexandr has agreed." They start making out after that, as my blood boils with rage.

My brother watches me cautiously, knowing what they are saying is absolute bullshit; she isn't fucking pregnant, and like fuck did I okay this crap!

Then *I* come into view, smirking.

"You both started without me?"

"Turn it off, Damian." I get up and go outside, stopping next to my Mercedes. My body won't stop trembling, and my ADHD is not helping my rage. I ball my hand into a fist and ram it into the car window, smashing the glass which slices through my hand. Blood drips onto the ground, but I don't give a fuck. I start to beat the shit out of my car, punch after punch, kick after kick, until my brother comes up behind me and restrains me.

"I get it, brother, trust me, I fucking get it, but think of the positive right now, yeah." I'm about to bite his head off because none of this has a positive fucking outcome. Clearly, she left me after seeing that fucking feed, and rightly so, but for the past five fucking months, I've been fucking the same two women, I've been fucking strippers, I've been plotting her death, and I've been fucking punishing her. I mean, fuck, I've got a fucking mistress!

I take a deep breath as Damian continues.

"We now know one or both of them are the ones who tried selling Phoebe to the Romanians, and I'm betting it was Selene's idea. She wants you, but she wants her grandmother's money more. We both know she wanted this alliance because she likes living a life of luxury, and Mindy, well, Mindy just wants a top man, and she's trying everything to get you, now that Sofia is back."

I nod and attempt to calm down as my brother lets go of me. I take a deep breath. "I need to contact Basil; Selene needs to have surveillance on her at all times, as well as Mindy."

Damian nods, squeezing my shoulder. "Make your call and get your hands cleaned and checked; we have your girl to find. Come to my office when you're done, yeah?

I have a feeling she stayed in America, knowing we would look in Europe."

I nod and whip my phone out, pulling up Basil's number. It rings three times before he answers.

"Alexandr, I still haven't found her," he states without saying hello. I know his not finding her yet is wearing him down, especially with the Romanians after her.

I take a deep breath, knowing he's going to be pissed. "I know why she ran; it's all my fault and Selene's."

He's quiet for a couple of minutes before he clears his throat.

"Tell me everything."

And I do.

five

Phoebe

WE'RE SITTING in the back of an Uber on the way to Kevin's bar in town, all dolled up. We've been going there at least once a week, and the food is to die for, especially their quarter-pounder beef burger with fries.

I'm sitting in the middle, between Abby and Oliver, and as Abby stated, she's wearing her skimpy black dress and red high heels, her hair is down, curled around her face with little makeup, while I'm wearing my purple lacy dress that shows the tattoo on my collarbone nicely. The tattoo of little black sparrows flying to freedom runs diagonally over my shoulder. It's sentimental for me and has absolutely nothing to do with Alex's nickname for me; Little Bird. If I say it repeatedly, I might even believe it.

I've got my black heels and elbow-length, fingerless gloves to hide the hideous scar on my arm. I stitched it up myself with the animal suturing, self-learn kit I had in my bag—not my greatest idea, but my *yia-yia* taught me to use whatever I had in hand when I need to. I have a little makeup on, and my bangs, which I had cut two months ago, along with the pink dye highlights, curl around my face, leaving the rest of my hair cascading down my back.

Oliver is gently drawing little circles on the inside of my thigh, and I try not to sigh aloud. There is no tingly feeling whatsoever. Fuck.

Abby nudges me and gives me a sympathetic smile, and I smile back.

We arrive at the bar fifteen minutes later, and climb out and head inside. Abby goes ahead of me while Ollie places his arm around my waist. I look up at him and smile while he winks and guides me through the door toward the bar.

Abby sighs next to me. "Look at how hot he is." She looks at me and asks, "Do you think there's such a thing as arm porn?" I giggle while Ollie shakes his head at us just as James comes over. "'Sup man, ladies, what can I get you?" Ollie orders for us while Abby literally drools all over the bar top, and my shoulders shake with silent laughter.

"Two cosmopolitans and a bud." James nods, his eyes lingering on Abby, and I smirk.

Once we have our drinks, Abby drags us to the little dance floor they have installed as "Die for You" by the Weeknd plays. Oliver grabs my hip and grinds against my ass. I can feel his erection, and yet, nothing; my lady bits don't even fucking flutter. I groan in frustration, and he grinds harder, misinterpreting my noise. Abby sees how uncomfortable I look and grabs my hand, pulling me to her as "Flowers" by Miley Cyrus plays. Oliver states he's going to get us more drinks, refusing to dance to this one, making us chuckle and nod. We sing and dance to about two songs when I look around for Oliver and notice he hasn't returned with our drinks, so I grab Abby's hand and drag her toward the bar.

"What's up?" She asks as I look around the bar, not seeing him anywhere. Ginny is currently serving people, so James must be on break. I frown at Abby. "Ollie was supposed to bring us drinks two songs ago, and I'm parched. Where is he?" She furrows her brows and looks around, too, then starts to drag me toward the bathrooms. "Let's check down here; maybe he's gone to the bathroom." I nod, and we head down to the right of the bar.

As we get to the men's bathroom at the end of the hall, we hear a grunting noise around the corner where the fire exit is. We look at each other and smirk, then tiptoe to have a look, giggling quietly.

As we turn the corner, we stop dead in our tracks, completely shocked and, honestly, a little sick. The bastard kissed me with that mouth only an hour ago.

Oliver is currently on his knees with James's cock in his mouth, deep-throating him while moaning, and his finger is deep in James's ass. *What the fuck!*

I look at Abby, and she looks back at me. She sighs, disappointed in this outcome, then crosses her arms over her chest and leans against the wall to enjoy the show.

I shake my head and turn to watch, too; another one bites the dust.

Men are fucking pigs, so maybe I should try women instead. I take out my phone and record them, knowing insurance is always good. Abby smirks at me, and I just shrug.

"Fuck, that's it, Ol. Suck my big meaty cock." James groans, and I bite my lip to stop laughing out loud while Abby puts her fist in her mouth, biting it. "Fuck, I need you in me, baby." James quickly removes his dick from Oliver's mouth, then turns around, sticking his ass out and shaking it, while my whole body shakes with silent laughter. I struggle to keep my phone still.

Oliver grabs a hold of Jame's hips and shoves his tongue deep into his ass, shooting bile into my throat. That tongue was *in my mouth* an hour ago.

Fuck, I feel sick.

Abby grabs my arm and squeezes it, knowing where my mind is drifting. I've basically tongued

James's ass. The thought sticks in my head, and I gag, making Abby snort. Oliver, who is completely unaware that we're here and that I'm about to vomit, gets up and bends over James, sticking his tongue out, licking around James's earlobe while he undoes his jeans, shucking them down a little, and taking his cock out.

Huh.

It's a lot smaller than I thought it was. I tilt my head to the side as Abby's body starts to shake with silent laughter, also noticing how small he is. I mean, would that even reach my hymen?

Oliver places his cock at James's asshole and rubs it over, bringing me out of my head as James states, "Fuck baby, don't tease me; shove it in. I want to feel you so badly." And he does what he's asked, thrusting his cock, hard, into James's ass, making him groan loudly. Oliver reaches around and grabs James's dick and starts jacking him off hard and fast, his hips thrusting faster in James's ass at the same time, and within four minutes and thirty-eight seconds—yes, I timed it—they both come. After James's cum spills in his hand, Oliver lifts it and runs his tongue through the cum, and this time I really do swallow my own vomit. He grabs James's dick again and slowly strokes it while I stop the recording and put my phone away, knowing I've got enough.

Oliver murmurs, "Fuck baby, I missed you in my ass; a week is too long to go without you." James sighs as he leans back against Oliver, who gently kisses his neck, and I lift a brow. Now, why has he been with *me* if he feels this way?

I'm about to open my mouth and ask because I would never stand between love, whether it's with the same sex or not, but he shocks the shit out of me.

"Not long to go, babe; tonight's the night I'll finally fuck her, then she should trust me to give me the details of where her grandmother's money is. Then, we can leave together."

James nods, tilting his head upward to find Oliver's mouth, and they start to make out. Oliver thrusts slowly, probably trying to get himself hard again. His hand is playing with James's cock, and they're both moaning.

I look at Abby, and her face is red with anger as well. This is why she's one of the only ones in this world I trust now; she has my back just like I have hers.

Heaving a dramatic sigh, I step forward. "Well, so much for losing my virginity tonight." I state just low enough that the two thieving lovebirds don't hear.

Abby responds, "And there goes my good dicking." We look at each other and laugh, causing both men's heads to shoot our way, gasping at the sight of us.

Oliver quickly pulls out of James, and they both pull their jeans up. "Phoebe, baby, it's not what it looks like, I—"

I cut him off. "So, you weren't fucking James's ass, declaring you wanted my money to run away together?" He shuts up and pales while I chuckle.

"How do you know about my grandmother's money, Oliver? Only my close family knows about it, so how on earth do you?" I inquire coldly, and he looks at James, who nods.

"Look, a man named Christian Baciu approached me four months ago and told me to get close to you. Someone tried selling you for $5 million, but he saw you and thought you were no longer pure or whatever, and offered us the $5 million if we got you to tell us the location of the $100 million." I freeze momentarily. I know that name; that's the Romanian mafia head. For a while now, I've known that my uncle tried to sell me, and instead of telling me, my father decided to keep me in the dark. It looks like someone else wants me gone, too. Probably Selene, which wouldn't surprise me; she and that slut *did* mention me getting picked up by them.

Oliver starts to walk over to me, taking my silence as permission when, really, I'm more dangerous than the Romanian he's been in contact with; he just doesn't know it yet. Only Abby, Juan, and my old guard, Colin, who is currently my spy in my family, know my true self. It looks like things are about to be different, and everyone will know.

I think it's time I come out of hiding.

As he walks toward me slowly, he states, "Maybe, you give *us* the $5 million now, then I can tell Christian that your sister has the money. Yeah, that sounds better, doesn't it? It's a win-win situation." He goes to put his hand, which still has cum over it, on my shoulder, and I quickly bend down, grabbing the knife that's strapped to my leg under my dress. I twist it so the length of the blunt side of the blade is against my arm while the sharp end goes to his throat, and he stops still, hands going up in surrender, swallowing hard.

I smirk. "Did you know there are over one hundred ways I could break your bones in your body without you dying?" He swallows again, and I can hear James's breath pick up.

"You're a pathetic little boy, not realizing who you are dealing with. Christian is a puppy compared to me." Abby chuckles. She, Juan, and Colin are the only ones who have seen this side of me. For the five years I lived with my father, I had to hide behind my mask, the quiet, shy girl that I used to be before I lived with Athena, and she, with the help of the Spanish Don, Juan Garcia, who happens to be my uncle, and whom my father didn't know about when he married my mother. Juan turned me into a lethal killing machine. However, I can't really call myself a killer…until recently.

I never had any practice because my *yia-yia* passed away, then my father took me back, which means I hadn't killed anyone until three months ago, when I walked outside of the library where Abby was supposed to meet me, and I heard screaming. I ran around the corner just in time to catch two dickheads trying to attack her. One held Abby while the other was undoing her pants as she tried to kick out at them. I grabbed my knife from my boot, and I ran toward them, stabbing the guy who was trying to undo her pants. The other guy paled when I slowly looked up at him; he held his hands up and backed away before taking off. I got my small pistol from the back pocket of my jean shorts, and shot him once in the back of his head.

I expected Abby to scream and run away from me, instead, she nearly toppled us to the ground while hugging me and crying. Nobody ever found out that I killed them, thanks to the technical skills my uncle taught me. As it turns out, several women came forward after seeing those men's faces plastered on

TV, claiming rape. The police didn't really try all that hard to find their killer. It makes me smirk every time I think about it, and now Abby trains with me every week. We do Judo on Saturdays, with a mix of martial arts and boxing, then we shoot at the shooting range one town over on Sundays, much to my Uncle Juan's happiness.

I contacted him after my first kill, and he decided to tell me all about the human traffickers. He said he was waiting for me to be ready, and hearing that they are now picking up children to sell, it was a no-brainer. He's given me over thirty-five targets in three months, and I've had perfect kill shots each time. They call me the Angel of Death, because, apparently, someone noticed I was a woman because of the shoes I was wearing when I went after a cartel drug runner, who had gone rogue trying his hand at trafficking. He tried to snatch a five-year-old little girl, and I had to do something to make my uncle proud. The person noticed nothing else about me. Some people say I need catching, and others are praising me because of who I kill.

But back to my grandmother's money and estate. I did offer my uncle half after I learned about it because it is more his than mine, but he declined, stating I earned it. He is the only other person I trust. I used to trust Sergi, but I know his loyalty would be with Alex, and that's why I haven't contacted him. The same is true of Sofia, no matter how much I miss them.

In front of me, standing beside the emergency exit, Oliver pales, and I sneer at him.

"You're one of the richest people I know, thanks to your parents' good luck in the real estate business, and yet you want to steal *my* grandmother's hard-earned money?" I smirk. "And I'm guessing it's because they won't approve of you two," I snarl, the fucking, lying piece of shit. I leave out that my *yia-yia's* money is mainly blood money, but he doesn't need to know that.

"Here's what you're going to do."

He tries to speak, and my knife slices him a little. Blood starts to drip from his neck, and he whimpers, causing James to sob. I roll my eyes, pussies the both of them.

This was the guy I was going to fuck Alex out of my system with? Geez.

"You're going to tell Christian that he was right; I'm not pure." Abby snorts, knowing it's bullshit. "Then you're going to request a meeting with him, and you're going to ensure that my father, Basil Adino, and Damian and Alexandr Volkov are present. You'll tell him you've gotten ahold of my inheritance. Do you understand?" He whimpers, most likely recognizing the names, and doesn't want to meet them. I roll my eyes again. "You're not actually going, you idiot, I am, but you're not to tell them that, got it?" He nods fast, causing him to cut himself more, whimpering in pain. I remove my knife from his throat, and James quickly grabs a hold of him and looks at me.

"We're sorry, Phoebe. We just didn't know what else to do."

I tilt my head, and as Abby states, "You were supposed to confide in your friend, and she most probably would have given you the money. Instead, you tried to manipulate her, ruin your friendship and trust, and use her. Now, you're on your own." I nod, agreeing, while both men's faces pale, realizing they fucked up because, before Oliver tried to be more, he was a good friend.

Abby grabs my hand, ready to pull me away, and I state, "You have twenty-four hours to get me the meet-up information. Betray me, and it won't be my knife next time, it'll be a bullet. They don't call me the Angel of Death for no reason." Their mouths drop, and they look ready to pass out.

Abby and I turn around and head out.

"Let's go home, yeah?" Abby says, and I nod, squeezing her hand. Yet another person betrayed me but, at least this time, I didn't drop my mask like I was starting to with Alex.

six

Alexandr

I'M SITTING in my office at Volkov & Co., going over our stock portfolio to ensure we're still on top, when my brother enters my office just as my phone rings. Damian sits on the couch along the opposite wall as I answer the phone.

"Alexandr," I answer. My eyebrows shoot up when I hear Basil on the other end, and my heart skips a beat. Maybe he's found her? Fuck, I hope so. I have some making up to do.

"Alexandr, how are you?"

I clear my throat. "I'm doing alright, Basil. What can I do for you?"

Damian's eyebrows shoot up as I talk. I put the call on speaker.

"I had an interesting call from Christian Baciu; we have been requested for a meeting with him and Damian in forty-eight hours at the old, abandoned warehouse on 9th Street. Apparently, some unknown person has managed to get a hold of my daughter's inheritance."

I shoot up from my seat while Damian's face goes stone cold, which would scare away the meanest criminals.

"Basil, it's Damian. How exactly did he manage to get a hold of Phoebe's trust?" he demands in a cold voice, and I clear my throat as a worried lump forms in my chest.

Damian can see the worry in my eyes.

Does this person have her?

If he does, I will fucking gut him.

"Apparently, a man he employed managed to trick her into falling for him; they were lovers, his words, not mine." I growl loudly as he sneers the sentence out, clearly pissed that his little girl has slept around. Someone else took what was mine, then again, if what Selene said was true, she's been doing this for years! Hypocritical, I know, but I don't give a fuck; her virginity was supposed to be *mine*! Her body was supposed to be *mine*!

Damian places his hand on my shoulder to keep me calm, but my rage is taking over.

"Selene also overheard the conversation and has insisted she join us."

I lost it.

I swipe all my equipment and paperwork to the floor, my chest feeling heavy. Selene doesn't give a shit about her sister; she's after the money, the greedy, fucking bitch!

"What time is the meeting? This could be a setup." Damian takes over while I try to calm myself.

Fucking Selene, she has been after the money for years.

"At 4:30. I have already got men scoping the place out, and yours are welcome to join, obviously."

Damian scowls but keeps his voice calm. "Sergi and two of my men will be there within the hour, and we'll arrive an hour before the scheduled time. We'll see you then." Then he hangs up and looks at me.

I shake my head and say, "I'm off to the club."

I start to walk out when Damian states, "You want her back, yet you still fuck around. How do you think she'll feel when she finds out? Learn from my mistakes, brother." I turn slightly and growl. "She's already fucking around, so it doesn't fucking matter, does it?" I walk out, skipping the elevators, and jog down the stairs, hoping it'll calm my thoughts.

Twenty minutes later, I'm pulling into the underground parking for our strip club. It wasn't that long ago that I had to stand and watch my brother try to forget his wife, and now I am basically doing the same. The difference is that she's not my fucking wife because she ran, and she's been intimate with others, so fuck her!

I know I am not thinking clearly, but I don't give a fuck right now.

After parking, I walk through the main doors and sit at the VIP table set aside for our family, and within minutes, Candy brought me my usual drink of scotch. She then straddles on my lap. I grin at her. This is what I needed to forget fucking everything. I take a big gulp of my drink, wanting to get wasted, while Candy swivels her hips, giving me a lap dance with a little *extra*.

We've been doing this over the last few months. I still meet up with Mindy and Selene to keep up pretenses and, let's face it, they're hot as fuck in the sack together. But mainly I come here, and Candy is my go-to girl; she was there for me after Phoebe left, and I owe her a lot, even if it was her job to give me a happy ending. She kept me sane; I've even gone as far as to provide her with a room at the Russo's hotel, the Preziosa, which she is elated about. I've made her my mistress, and she's perfect for it. And two months ago, our doctor came and give her the contraceptive shot. There's nothing better than seeing my cum drip out of her cunt. When we fulfill contract, which we will, and since Phoebe has already signed it, she'll just have to get used to Candy. She'll be around a lot.

I know Phoebe's leaving was my fault, but after finding out she's been fucking around, I don't feel guilty anymore. I was going to dismiss Candy, but now this will be Phoebe's punishment for giving her body to someone else, and I don't give two fucks if I sound hypocritical.

Candy grinds down on my cock that, after thinking of Phoebe, is now paying attention, and is getting harder as Candy takes off her lacy, pink bra, her fake tits falling out. My mouth waters, and very slowly, I lean forward and use the tip of my tongue to nudge her pebbled nipple. She jolts, and I smirk, taking her whole nipple in my mouth. I nip it a little with my teeth before rubbing my tongue around it, then suck hard. She moans, grabbing my hair, and I move to do the same to the other one. I slowly kiss up her neck, sucking a little, leaving my mark, like I always do with her, and then find her mouth.

She dives her tongue into my mouth, and I rip off her thong. She undoes my jeans and reaches for my hard cock, stroking it, before she lifts it a little and uses her hand to guide it toward her entrance. She slowly slides down my cock, moaning. I grip her hips and groan. She's not tight, but she still feels nice, warm, and wet. I lift her, then slam her back down, and my mouth attaches to her nipple. One hand holds her hip while my other holds my scotch as she fucks herself on me. She finally feels tighter as she comes, and once she does, she gets off me and takes my cock into her mouth. I groan as she deep throats me again and again and again, all while swallowing. I come within minutes, with a picture of Phoebe in my mind.

Fuck, that was good.

Candy gets up and straddles me again, kissing me like her life depends on it, and I groan into the kiss, tasting myself while her hips swivel again. When we pull apart, I move her hair out of her eyes and kiss her nose while she smiles sweetly back at me. See, perfect, and at least she is here. I do not give a fuck if I'm a hypocrite.

"I missed you, handsome," she says in her whiny, little voice, but I ignore it as usual.

"Sorry, baby, business." She nods, then kisses me again, grinding her pussy on me and managing to get me hard for a second time. This time though, I move her onto her back, chucking my glass on the floor, and thrust into her ass, fucking her hard and fast as two of my fingers push into her wet cunt. A few minutes later, she comes, screaming my name as her ass tightens around me. Her pussy flutters against my digits, and I groan, coming into her ass.

I place my face into her neck, suckling gently, and say, "Come on, baby, I want more of you." She giggles in a high-pitched giggle that I again ignore and get dressed, and we head out to her hotel room, where I get my fill, until I have to leave for the meeting.

Forty-eight hours later, Damian, Sergi, and I are at the warehouse. They've checked it several times over while I had my sex-fest, much to their dismay, especially Sergi, but I just shrug at him. He's barely said two words to me lately.

We couldn't find any traps, but our men are spread out, just in case. Basil has already gone inside with his guard and daughter.

Damian looks at me. "You ready?" I nod, and we walk into the warehouse with Sergi behind us. As we walk through the door, Christian and his right-hand man, Mihai, come out of the shadows where we knew he was.

He says, "Welcome, gentlemen."

I roll my eyes while Sergi states, "What are we doing here, Christian? This has nothing to do with us. Alexandr and Phoebe's contract is void; it has been for months." I grind my teeth; it's not fucking void, because Mindy is not fucking pregnant. Sergi knows this; he looks at me and smirks, the fucker. I shake my head.

Christian smiles and says, "I agree, but for some reason, my man on the inside insisted Damian and Alexandr be here. I'm guessing you're here as a backup."

Sergi just shrugs as Basil speaks, "Where is my daughter?"

Christian just laughs. "I haven't got a fucking clue. My man on the inside sought me out through an ad I placed for anyone wanting to earn money. He told me about a girl he was trying to seduce because he had overheard her and her friend talk about what to do with her inheritance, and how she had over a hundred million. When he said her name, it sounded very familiar, and when he showed me a picture of her, well, as you can tell, I agreed. I originally wanted the girl until my informant told me she wasn't pure. So, now, I figure, the money would be better."

I can feel my rage start to flow again.

"And where is your informant?" I demand coldly, not wanting to discuss Phoebe and the men she's been with. Again, I know it's hypocritical, but I don't fucking care. Christian frowns, realizing his informant is not here yet.

Suddenly, a huge crash shakes the room as glass from the roof comes crumbling down. We all jump back as someone drops down. I pull my gun simultaneously with everyone else, ready to fire, until I see who came crashing down.

Wearing black leather pants and a matching leather crop top, showing a tattoo on her collarbone, biker boots on her feet, her hair down in waves with pink highlights, and looking even more beautiful than the first day I met her is my girl. Fuck, my heart beats erratically in my chest as Selene gasps and Basil chokes in shock.

"Phoebe?"

But she doesn't pay them attention; she focuses solely on me. She tilts her head to the side, her bright green eyes calculating, and then she smirks as we all stand there staring at her with our mouths hanging open.

Finally, I hear her sweet voice again, but instead of loving, it's cold, void of emotion.

"*Geia sou, agápi mou*, missed me?" Her father and Selene suck in a breath, obviously knowing what she was saying, but yet again, I didn't learn her fucking language as she did mine. My brother clears his throat, and I look at him, his eyes wide, looking into mine while Sergi tenses at her words. They understood what she said, too, fuck.

She gets my attention again, and my heart stops at her next words, showing how stupid I am for not realizing she clearly kept an eye on everyone, including me.

"How's Candy today? Still tucked in nice and cozy in the hotel room you bought her in Russo's hotel. Or did you drop her off at work where you like to fuck her regularly?" She smirks, and I can't breathe. Who is this woman? Christian laughs, now out of his stupor, taking her attention off of me. Damian places a hand on my shoulder as the guilt I suppressed over having a mistress begins to fire up inside me, and followed closely behind is the horrible realization that the feelings I thought I felt for Candy are non-existent.

She was something to pass the time. Pain shoots through me as I mutter, "Fuck," while Damian squeezes my shoulder again, knowing I've realized what he's known for months now…because he's been there.

I've literally dug my own grave. And Phoebe is waiting to bury me in it.

seven

Phoebe

I'M WALKING down the steps from my general chemistry laboratory class when I bump into Abby. She's grinning madly at me, and I raise a brow at her.

"Sorry, it's just, right now, you're that quiet, shy girl, but when we get home, you're going to turn into this badass bitch in leather. I just love the transformation." She smirks, and I try to match her giddiness but just can't.

Don't get me wrong, I'm not ungrateful for all I've learned from my grandmother and uncle, but sometimes I wish I was still that naïve little girl, who didn't know evil in the world exists, and her mother still puts her to bed.

"I never used to be like this, Abs. I *was* that quiet, shy girl until I lived with Athena." Abby gives me a sad smile.

"I know, but think of it this way, if you weren't this badass bitch, then what happened a few months ago would have been worse."

I smile at her, giving her a side hug, and then drag her toward my car to stop this conversation. Her nightmares return when she talks about them, and I'm not going to be there tonight to help her through them.

I have twenty-four hours to reach my destination and scope it out without being seen. My uncle supplied a plane for me and made sure my Harley Davidson is waiting for me at the airstrip. I only kept the Buick to keep up the pretenses.

Abby and I get home half an hour later, and I go pack. I don't have classes tomorrow, so it's not too bad, but Abby will stay behind because it's too dangerous. I won't risk her. She comes into my room, helps me pack a bag, and takes it out to my car.

She gives me a tight hug and says, "Go kick some ass."

I chuckle, get into my car, and head to my uncle's plane, just outside of town, on an old airstrip that hasn't been used in years.

Five and a half hours later, we're landing in New York. Once business here is done, I'll be home in California for a few days, and then I'll have to return New York to fulfill the contract Uncle gave me last week. I just want to have some fun first. I smirk.

I get off the plane, strap my bag to the back of my bike, and check my watch. It's 11 PM. The meeting is tomorrow afternoon. Oliver was shitting himself when he told me. I shake my head. What the fuck was

I thinking, letting someone like that take my virginity? Fucking glad I didn't.

I power up my baby and rev her with a grin on my face. I've missed my bike. I only use it for missions. She's matte black, has dark purple shadow painted on the tank, and it matches my personality; dark with color hidden on the inside.

I speed away from the hangar, and head to my uncle's house in Brooklyn. Colin will meet me there.

Forty minutes later, I'm pulling up to the iron gates, and the guard lets me in. Colin is waiting for me by the steps. I grin when I see him, and, instead of a bear hug like I usually get, he tells me off like I'm ten years old again, making me chuckle.

"Where is your helmet, *ángelos*?" He has a scowl on his face, his dark brown eyes full of worry.

I shake my head and get off my bike. I head toward him and hug him tight. "I'm fine, Colin." He squeezes me tighter while lifting me slightly off the ground, and I smile. I wish he were my father. I often wished my mother hadn't loved my father so much, but she *did* love him, and she didn't stray.

"How was your flight?" he asks.

"It was alright. So, what do I need to know for tomorrow?" I get right into it, making him chuckle.

"Christian is bringing his second in command and fifteen men. Damian and Alexandr are both going, and Alexandr is currently at the Preziosa with his mistress Candy, who owes twenty thousand dollars to the cartel for drugs, mainly cocaine. I'm unsure if Alexandr knows, but I have proof that she's swiping money from Russian businesses from his phone. Your father is still going tomorrow, but your sister has decided she wants to attend as well." He smiles at the last bit, and I end up grinning, making him chuckle.

"Tomorrow will be fun."

He nods. "Indeed, your uncle has also called; there are three men caught up in trafficking. They've targeted children between the ages of three and six on the east side of Brooklyn from the Bratva, but Damian is unaware because these men are low on the food chain, except for Grigoriy. He's a *sovietnik* and the front runner for finding the young girls or boys in group homes. The two lower-level men, unknown names, picks up the kids, then takes them to the meeting point for the Mexican cartel to pick up."

My face turns to fire. Fucking *kids*! Seriously? I look at Colin, and he nods. After I anonymously provided the Bratva with the information about their missing kids, I said I'd give them one week to find their traitors, but I won't be able to, and Colin knows this. He hands me the files to go through.

I put my bag in my bedroom, and then I spend an hour and a half going through the files, before I head out to scope out the warehouse. I look at my watch. 1:30 AM. Fifteen hours to go.

After returning at 7 AM, I get a quick nap and some food, before going over my plans again for the fifth time. Colin watches me; he will only intervene if he thinks it's necessary.

I get ready with two hours to spare, knowing they'll all get there early to check the place again. When I was there before, several men came and went, checking for traps.

I leave my hair down, and wear my leather pants and crop top with biker boots. I make sure I have knives in both boots, and my handgun with a silencer in the back of my pants. I place four throwing stars in the safety pocket on my top, before I look in the mirror and smirk.

"Let's party."

Forty-five minutes later, after I've hugged Colin goodbye, I arrive at the warehouse. Men are everywhere, just like I predicted. Still, after watching them for a few hours, I know none of them will look behind the warehouse to the right-hand side of the building, because it's a tight fit. After leaving my bike in plain sight, to distract them, I slowly make my way over, chuckling, while I stay out of sight. Then I climb the thin ladder I placed there last night. Once on the roof, I crawl, and get into position near the skylight. I already cut around the glass last night, so all I have to do is throw the rock and smash through it. It should break easily.

Twenty minutes after I'm in place, Christian and Mihai arrive, and move to the shadows. I roll my eyes; how predictable. Five minutes later, my father, his most trusted guard, Peter, and my beloved sister enter. I squeeze my hand into a fist, trying not to reach for my gun. The fucking bitch is selling me to pay off her habits. When Colin told me that, I fucking snapped and broke my favorite table at my uncle's house, which happened to be the only fucking thing I liked there.

Ten more minutes go by, and in walks the Volkovs and Sergi, who, let's face it, is basically a Volkov as well. I stay hidden, waiting for one of them to ask where Christian's informant is. Yeah, *informant*. New information Colin provided. Oliver told me *he* was approached, not that *he* as the one to reach out to *them*. The dick-less, spineless bastard is so getting his neck split open when I see him.

Finally, after going back and forth, Alexandr asks where Christian's informant is, and they start looking around for him. I smirk and grab the rock before getting to my knees, and smashing the stone through the glass. It breaks easily. I get to my feet, push myself over the edge, keeping my legs bent, and land perfectly crouched. I smirk, then straighten, my eyes going straight to Alexandr, ignoring everyone else in the room, but keeping them in my line of sight.

I keep my voice cold, showing him who I really am.

"*Geia sou, agápi mou*, missed me?" My father and Selene suck in a breath, knowing what I just said, while Sergi stills, and by the looks of things, his brother also recognized what I said, but as usual, Alexandr still hasn't learned my language. He looks at his brother with wide eyes, and I decide to play with him a little.

"How's Candy today? Still tucked in nice and cozy in the hotel room you bought her at Russo's hotel. Or did you drop her off at work where you like to fuck her regularly?" I smirk. Does it hurt that he took a mistress who happens to be a coke-headed stripper? Yes, it fucking kills. Am I going to let him know this? Hell no, plus it didn't fucking help when I tried to move on. Not only did I not feel anything down below for the guy, but he turned into a spineless weasel who preferred dick.

Christian laughs, now out of his stupor, and I turn toward him with a cold and calculating smile.

"Fuck," I hear Alex mutter.

Yeah, you fucked up, you dickhead.

"Well, if it isn't the infamous Phoebe Adino." Christian states happily.

"Well, a little birdy says you've been after me." I spread my arms wide, holding them out. "Here I am! What are you going to do about it?" I smirk, baiting him, and his smile disappears, not liking me challenging him, especially with all these men as witnesses. Just when I hoped I'd have fun, he lifts a finger in the air, and a beast of a man comes running toward me from the left. I hear one coming from behind me, while another comes out from the shadows behind Christian. I smile wide, making him furrow his brows.

Finally, let's bring the Angel of Death out to play.

Time to show everyone who they're fucking with!

eight

Alexandr

I LOOK at Phoebe and Christian as they start talking, shucking my surprise with a shake of my head.

My heart thunders in my chest. What is she doing?

"Well, if it isn't the infamous Phoebe Adino." Christian states happily while Phoebe replies cockily.

"Well, a little birdy says you've been after me." She spreads her arms, holding them out at her sides. "Here I am! What are you going to do about it?" She smirks, baiting him, and his smile disappears.

He lifts a finger in the air, and a man comes running toward her from our side, another one coming from behind her, while another comes out from the shadows behind Christian. And she smiles. She fucking *smiles*. I'm about to intervene, not wanting her hurt when I hear Selene fucking giggle behind her hand, trying to disguise it as a cough, the bitch.

I go to step forward, but before we can do anything, Phoebe sidekicks the man in the chest, and he goes skidding across the floor, landing on his back. Sshe bends down and grabs a knife from her boot, making my brow's shoot up, and all of us men stare at her in shock. Christian takes a step forward, confused when she takes the knife in her right hand, flips it so the safety part of the blade leans against her arm, and slices across the next guy's neck, all while putting her left hand in her top, grabbing a fucking throwing star, and throwing it behind her. The star hits straight between the guy's eyes.

She turns and smirks at the guy she kicked. She lifts her arms to the side, mocking him. "What are you waiting for? Come and get me, *choíros*."

I go to walk forward, disbelieving what I am seeing, but both Damian and Sergi stop me, grabbing my arms.

"Let's see what she's got, brother."

I scowl at him; he looks too fucking intrigued by this. Peter, Basil's trusted guard, is holding him back as well.

The big guy runs at Phoebe again, clearly trying to use his body to knock her down, but she side steps him and ducks under his arms, and then...she giggles. Fucking *giggles*!

"Is she fucking enjoying this?" Sergi asks in shock, while Basil frowns at his daughter, all while I'm fucking stumped. Christian holds up another finger, and another guy comes out from the shadows, and both Damian and Sergi let go of me. All three of us go to intervene, with the guy coming up fast from behind her. We stop short when she gets another fucking throwing star from her top and throws it behind her, hitting him in the neck. He chokes on his own blood and grabs the star, pulling it out—a rookie mistake. I shake my head as he dies on the spot. We all look at Phoebe in shock, and Christian's mouth is hanging open.

"Well, that wasn't very nice. Here I thought you wanted to play fair, you know, with me being a 'girl' and all that." She uses her fingers to make air quotes, but she doesn't sound out of breath. "So now I get to play by my rules, and I love playing by mine." She smirks, then runs up to the big guy, who has paled.

Catching him off guard, she jumps up, wrapping her legs around his neck. His grabs her legs, trying to pry them apart, but she just chuckles—fucking *chuckles*, then grabs hold of his thick neck and twists it. We all hear a crack as the guy's legs give out, killed instantly. She drops with him, but her feet land on the floor, and she stands straight, wiping her pants before looking at Christian with the biggest fucking smirk going, tilting her head.

I look at Damian, and he looks back at me in shock, while Sergi's mouth hangs open. I can see Selene in my side view; she's gone pale. Basil just stares at the woman he thought was his daughter. I know it's not the fucking time, but my dick likes what he's seeing, while my fucking heart aches at what she's become.

Has she always been like this? Was she hiding her true self?

"Tell me something, Christian. Have you ever heard of the Shadow?" I still, and so does every other man in this room.

Christian pales slightly but states coldly, "No offense, little girl, but I doubt you are it."

Phoebe laughs. "Of course, I'm not her, though that would be a great honor, don't you think? No, the Shadow was my grandmother, Athena Angelos, Angelos being her maiden name, by the way." She looks at her father briefly before looking back at Christian, and stating, "Her married name was Athena Garcia." She smiles widely, and I furrow my brows. Garcia, as in the Spanish Mafia Garcia? I look at Damian, and he seems as confused as me.

Basil speaks up, finally finding his voice, "No, Phoebe, you are mistaken; your grandmother and mother have no relation to the Garcias. Juan Garcia will not be happy that you're using his name. I don't know how you learned the things you did, but lying is not acceptable." He tries to state it carefully, not wanting to have a star chucked at his head, and I shake my head.

Phoebe just smiles and gets out her phone and dials a number, and all of a sudden, Juan Fucking Garcia's voice comes through the speakers.

"What can I do for you, *Princesa*?" he asks, and Basil pales, and I see Sergi stiffen. I frown at his reaction.

"It would seem my father does not believe you are my uncle."

He laughs through the phone. "Have you given up some of your secrets, my dear?"

Phoebe smiles widely. "Only about you and Athena."

I step forward, gaining her attention.

She looks me in the eyes as she states to her uncle, "You're on-speaker, *Tio*. Why don't you clue these small-minded people, who I'm currently shocking the shit out of, in about how you and my grandmother, the Shadow, trained me to be from the age of ten?"

I freeze, realizing what she's insinuating. The Shadow trains assassins, and there's no fucking way my girl was taught to be one, not my quiet, shy fucking fiancée, and certainly not by her sweet, old grandmother, from the age of fucking 10!

"No, no," Basil says, just as Juan states, "Well, darling girl, we trained you to be one of the best assassins in the world, and you are, despite having to go back to your father's. You have killed over fifty people in the last three months alone, and I'm now guessing more. It seems you've most likely killed some of the Romanians. You are not only my most prized weapon but also my loving niece, isn't that right, my Angel of Death?"

Phoebe smirks, and I hear several inhaled breaths as most of the men in the room back away from her, realizing who we are all dealing with. And I swear I can hear Sergi growl. I look at him again, and he looks murderous. What the fuck? I look back at Phoebe, and I shake my head. She's not her; she's not the woman who has assassinated traffickers, gaining the title of the 'Angel of Death,' no way, not my girl.

"No, no, no! You are not her!" Basil shouts, and Phoebe looks at him.

"Unfortunately, Father, this is what happens when you send me away to keep me safe. Safe? Huh. You sent me to an assassin training school." Then she tells Juan, "I'll call you once I'm done, *Tio*. We need to discuss the information you gave my contact regarding the traffickers. I'll be done soon."

She hangs up her phone, placing it back in a small pocket in her leather pants. I take a step forward again, but Damian grabs my arm. I scowl at him, but he shakes his head.

I snap, "You cannot expect me to stand here and watch!" I hiss in a low whisper.

Damian leans over and whispers back, "We're not dealing with your sweet, shy fiancée, Al, we're dealing with the Angel of fucking Death! She shoved a guy's cock down his own throat after cutting it off herself two weeks ago. She can handle herself, and, if she needs us, then we'll get involved, but at the moment, I think us getting in her way will piss her off, and you'll lose your chance. As it stands, she already knows about your mistress; who's to say she doesn't know about Selene, too?" I pale at his words. Fuck. I stand back a bit, concerned for my own dick, making Damian snort, and I narrow my eyes at him.

Shit, my woman is going to castrate me.

I look back at Phoebe, and her attention is now on Christian. She pulls a gun from the back of her pants, and before Christian can even sneeze, she has it pointed at his head.

"Mihai, in moments, you will receive proof of Christian embezzling money from your men without their knowledge. He is also embezzling money from both the Russian and Greek Mafia, and as agreed by the council of elders, the punishment for treason is death," she states coldly. We are all still confused at how he managed to embezzle money from our businesses that he has no take in, and how the fuck does Phoebe know about the elders?

She continues, despite our confusion, "Proof is also being sent to the heads of both organizations. You, Mihai, are now the head of the Romanians, and I expect within the next twenty-one days, you will make sure all trafficking of flesh has stopped. If not, I will be back for you."

Christian steps forward, forgetting about the gun pointed at his head.

"Listen here, you little bitch you—" He doesn't get to finish his sentence because she shoots a perfect shot right between his eyes. He flops onto the ground, and we all look at the woman I love more than anything, who I've tried to forget, as she smirks.

She looks at us and says, "Well, this was a fun time, but I have things to do and people to see." She then looks at Selene as Basil steps toward his eldest daughter. Phoebe just shakes her head at him. "I'm just going to make this perfectly clear, about why I have come out of hiding. I am *not* for sale. Try something like this again, and what I've just done today will seem like child's play. Do I make myself clear?" Nobody says a word; she still has her gun in her hand, dangling, and her eyes are trained on Selene, who stands there looking pale, her body shaking. Basil puts an arm around her, and I shake my head. What a fucking idiot!

Selene takes too long to answer.

"Do I make myself clear, Selene?" she shouts, causing Selene's body to jerk. Finally, she nods frantically. Phoebe looks at her father and states, "Always protecting her, even when you know she tried to sell me for her own gain, for her drugs. You always forget you had another daughter who needed you more. You're a pathetic man. *Nonos tis Nychtas* doesn't suit you!" Basil's face goes red while we all stay silent. She looks toward Mihai, who bows his head slightly out of respect. Then she turns to leave, completely ignoring me, Sergi, and Damian, which surprises me because she was closest with Sergi. I look at him, and he looks gutted.

I sigh because I know I'm the cause of their fractured friendship; she knew he'd be by my side because, despite not sharing blood, we're brothers. She stops just at the door, looking over her shoulder slightly.

"Damian?" Sergi and I freeze, and he clears his throat.

"What can I do for you, *Mladshaya Sestra*?" I clench my hands into fists when I notice her flinch at his words, but she continues while fucking ignoring me.

"You have twenty-four hours to uncover the three men in your organization who have affiliated themselves with human trafficking of 3- to 6-year-old children. The children live in group homes. If not, I will take over the task. Your clock is ticking." Then she exits, leaving my brother reeling from the information that we have traitors among us.

To Peter, I hear Basil say, "Follow her, but at a safe distance; we've all heard the stories of the Angel of Death. Find out where she's living."

I mutter, "Fuck this," and follow her out while Damian calls for me, but I ignore him. When I get outside, she is already waiting for me, clearly knowing I'd follow. She's sitting astride a matte black Harley Davidson, with some dark purple blended into it, and no fucking helmet.

She looks sexy as fuck, though.

I cross my arms over my chest. "You have a contract to fulfill Phoebs."

She chuckles, then starts the bike up.

"I mean, Phoebe, you can't escape it. Our wedding was supposed to be last week."

She just shakes her head. "I don't think so, Alex. I heard you enjoyed what was supposed to be the start of our honeymoon with a couple of strippers." I flinch. "Why don't you get back to your mistress? She should be finished with her coke dealer on the couch in your office right about now. You and I are done. Maybe you shouldn't have fucked my sister; I might have stupidly forgiven you for the other slut, but you crossed a line. Now, if you'll excuse me, I have people to see. Also…why don't you ask your brother what I've been calling you for over a year?" She smirks, then drives off, leaving me in shock, and my body trembles with rage.

I grab my phone and click on the camera for my office, and lo and behold, Candy is leaning over my fucking couch, and some greasy, fat guy is fucking her bare from behind.

Shit.

I quickly text our doctor, needing tests done, and then I throw my phone against the warehouse, smashing it angrily.

My brother comes to stand beside me.

"My love," Damian says.

I turn around, feeling fucking dirty and pissed.

Not knowing what he's talking about, I snap, "What?"

He sighs. "What she called you in there—what she *has been* calling you for over a year—is my love."

I slowly close my eyes. Guilt builds in my chest, sucking the air from my lungs.

No, fuck no!

nine

Phoebe

I MAKE it back to my uncle's place in record time. Colin is now back at my father's to keep up pretenses. I must have only been here for twenty minutes when there was a knock on the front door. I sighed, unsurprised that I was followed, and opened it without a care to the world.

"You know you should at least have a knife, gun, or hell, even a fucking frying pan aimed at my head; I could be a cold-blooded killer." I shake my head, of course.

"You *are* a cold-blooded killer, Sergi." He chuckles, and I step to the side to let him in. He places a kiss on my head. "Let me guess, you want names."

He sighs. "Phoebe Pie, you and I were close, and no matter how long you've been gone, we will always be close; we have been for years. I'm still pissed that you left without saying a word to me, but I have always had your back, way before your father switched out the contract with you and your sister." I let out a sad chuckle. I knew he'd find it hard with me leaving without a trace.

Once a month since I was five, we'd meet up for ice cream with our mothers, and even after I had to leave, he would call me frequently. We continued our tradition when I returned, never telling him what I'd been trained to do. I always felt guilty, like I was lying to my best friend, but I pushed it aside. He used to bring Mila, too, when Sofia returned home. Alex used to hate it, but that's only because he was fighting for his best uncle title.

"You won the title yet?" I question him as we go to the gold and silver kitchen. It's hideous, but my uncle thinks it's funny because my aunt hates it. He loves her but loves winding her up more.

Sergi sits on the stool while looking around, and I get him a bottle of water and set beside him. "Not yet, but I will." I chuckle again, but a lump forms in my throat when he states, "You're still her favorite. She misses you."

A lone tear falls, and I wipe it away. I miss her, too.

He changes the subject, knowing the guilt I probably hold for not saying bye to the gorgeous little darling.

"Angel of Death?" he asks, and I sigh. I knew he wouldn't be happy about it.

"What do you want to know?" I question.

"Why didn't you tell me? All these years, we all thought you were this shy, quiet girl."

I look out the doorway toward the gardens and state, "I *was* that girl, Sergi, until my father sent me away when my mother was killed, and when I came back, I still trained behind my father's back, just not as much, so that girl came back a little each day. Alex helped to make me feel normal, but the day I got that link...." I looked at him, showing him my pain. He knew how much I loved Alex, and how deeply it tore me apart, and his eyes showed his own sorrow. "It was like the assassin jumped straight back in, my emotions shut off, and I was no longer that girl anymore. Heck, I didn't even make my first kill until three months ago, when two men tried to rape my best friend." He leans forward, elbows resting on the side, eyes contently on me. "She was waiting for me to get out of the library. I heard her scream and ran toward her. One guy was holding her down while the other was trying to undo her pants. It was like a switch being flipped. I sliced the one guy's throat, and I shot the other in the back of his head when he tried to run. Since then, with Juan's help, I've done my damn hardest to get rid of rapists and traffickers."

Sergi drops his head to his hands and sighs; I know talking about Juan is difficult for him.

"The three traitors?"

I sigh. I know he doesn't want to talk about Juan, and I know this was partially the reason why he came, why he followed me back here; he knew I'd be staying here, and he most likely didn't tell Damian or Alex. He knows I don't like lying to him, and if anyone can talk to me, it's him; he's my pseudo-brother and blood cousin.

I get up and head to the living area, picking up the folder and I handing it to him. "If this was Damian or Alex, I wouldn't be handing this to them; I was going to handle this myself, but I know how much you love dishing out pain to scum, especially traitors in your own organization."

He smiles at me, making his eyes light up.

I have missed him.

I continue to explain while he reads the information, getting more pissed by the second. I round the counter again and lean against it, my arms folded. "I have proof that there are three men into trafficking. They are targeting children between the ages of 3 and 6 on the east side of Brooklyn. All the men are Bratva, though they are low on the food chain, except for Grigoriy; he's a sovietnik, and the one tasked with finding the kids in group homes. The two lower-level men, unknown names, pick them up from either foster homes or group homes, then take them to the drop off point for the Mexican Cartel or the Romanians to pick up. There is also information on Alex's m-mistress Candy. She's been using him, and has managed to take $3 million from your businesses, undetected." I struggle with the last part; it still hurts that he has a mistress, while I'm still a fucking virgin. He's been living his best life like I meant nothing to him, while my body doesn't want anyone but him. I'm bound by him.

Sergi slams his hands down on the counter and shouts, "Fuck!" before he looks at me. "I'll sort this one, I promise." I smile and nod, knowing he means his word.

"Good, I have classes tomorrow that I really cannot afford to miss. I was going to return in a few days to get rid of the traitors, but they have a meeting at midnight tonight."

His eyebrows shoot high into his hairline. "You're still doing your veterinary courses?"

I smile and nod, and he hugs me tight, rasping, "I'm proud of you, Phoeb."

I squeeze him tighter and say, "I've missed you, Sergi."

He gives me a sad smile.

"This isn't goodbye, Phoebe; you're not disappearing on me again, you hear? You're like my little sister. Now, I have to go and get our money back, and inform Damian of everything you've shared with me. I expect our normal weekly phone call."

I chuckle and nod while he starts to walk out of the room, and I clear my throat. He knows what I am about to say and beats me to it.

He turns slightly and says, "I'm not ready to formally meet him yet, cuz. Denying your child, and leaving the mother to struggle and have to depend on others, only to try and get in touch again after twenty-nine years? It wasn't right. The only good thing about everything was having you as family. Just...just tell him to give me time." He sighs, and I nod. "I know, Sergi and, if it helps, I know he regrets it, especially after Aunt Valeria ripped into him when she saw you last year in the background while I was FaceTiming her. I believe he's still sleeping on the couch, and she blames him for keeping her child from her, even though you're not biologically hers. She sees you as hers...so just think about it." He gives me a sad smile, walks back up to me, wraps his arms around me, and squeezes me tight, before he kisses my head, then he leaves.

I wipe away a tear. Sergi has struggled a lot with his birth father. I just hope they get to figure it all out. Uncle Juan is actually an alright guy for a Don; he just made the wrong decision at the time.

I look at my watch. Shit, I have fifty minutes to get to the airstrip.

I quickly grab my bag and head back to my bike to strap it on, then I head to my uncle's plane.

As soon as I'm seated, I text Abby.

Me: now back on the plane; see you in about 7 hours.

She texts back instantly, making me chuckle.

Abby: good! The fucking goose is back again!

I burst out in laughter; I'm the only one able to contain Goosy.

She sends me a picture, and it's of Goosy and Ares having a face-off with a window between them. Goosy has his wings spread wide while Ares' hair stands up on his back. I lose it to a fit of laughter again. I can't wait to get home and not think about Alex for at least forty-eight hours. I sigh and lean my head back against the seat.

Home.

ten

Alexandr

I'M PACING my brother's living room, fucking pissed at myself, at Phoebe, at the world, and at fucking Sergi for disappearing for two fucking hours when we need to come up with a fucking plan.

I need to throw something; I eye the crystal vase on the table just as Sofia shouts, "Don't even think about it, Alexandr!" Damian chuckles while I grunt and sit next to him on his sofa.

"We need a fucking plan. Where has Sergi gotten to? I have shit to do!" I grunt out.

Damian raises an eyebrow at me. "You mean shit like confronting your mistress and checking yourself for diseases, because we both know you haven't been wrapping with her, or shit like going to Basil because we know he had a guy follow her, and find where your now ex-fiancée lives and stalk her?"

Sofia chuckles, and I glare at her, making her giggle like a girl. "I wouldn't look at me like that, Alexandr. Just because the brute there knocked me up again doesn't mean I can't smack some sense into you. What on earth were you thinking, making a coke addict stripper your mistress?" I go to defend myself.

I know I messed up. I know the reasons why I took Candy as a mistress were weak....

But Sofia is not done reaming my ass.

"I don't care how many happy endings she gave you when Phoebe left; she left for a good fucking reason; you've been sleeping with her sister, *her fucking sister*, behind her back, and you expected her to say, 'Oh, don't worry, love, I forgive you?' How many fucking times have you hit your head? Then you go and make that slut your mistress because she took 'care of you,' and you try to act like Phoebe leaving was out of the blue. How fucking stupid are you? I mean, come on, you know Phoebe, we all do; she wouldn't have just run off for the sake of running off, she would have had a good fucking reason. And not once did you think, 'oh, maybe she found out about the other women.'" She uses her fingers to quote the last bit of what she said, and I go to defend myself again because I did think maybe she knew, but Sofia chuckles so darkly that even Damian leans away from her a little.

Pregnant Sofia is a scary Sofia.

"Or, let me guess, you did think that but, instead, thought, 'no, she'll never find out about that' like us women are some dumb fucking cunts. If that were me, I wouldn't touch you with your brother's dick! For the last two months, you have acted like you had a right to fuck those women and get a mistress because, to you, it's her punishment for leaving when *you're* the one who was fucking her own sister like it wouldn't matter to her, so do you want to know what I think?"

Oh shit, I look around to see if I can make a run for it. I fucking hate it when Sofia says it like it is. Damian snorts when he sees me looking toward the kitchen archway, and I glare at him while Sofia continues, "I think you should leave poor Phoebe alone. Go put a ring on your mistress, or Selene instead; neither of them would mind your manwhore ways because seems as though *you can't keep it in your pants*." She shouts the last bit, and I stare at her with wide eyes while Damian clears his throat, wanting not to anger his hormonal, pregnant wife. When she was pregnant with Maksim, she threw a meat cleaver at him for complaining about having a sore back. He ducked just in time, and then she proceeded to cry her eyes out because she could have killed him, while he mumbled how glad he was that he missed the mood swings with Mila…but not quietly enough. I stood there in the kitchen in stitches and watched while she grabbed his glass of scotch and threw it at him. He slept on the sofa for about a week.

"*Malyshka*, this thing with Candy and Selene, while completely wrong, which he understands now, he was just trying to forget Phoebe because she hurt him, broke his heart. He fucked up, he knows this, give him a break, yeah?" he states calmly, and I look at him again with wide eyes, like he has a fucking death wish.

Her scowl has gotten scarier, her eyes narrow, and Damian swallows hard, probably regretting coming to my aid now. "Well, that's okay, then, isn't it? I mean, that's exactly what you did, right, darling?" she sneers.

Oh shit, she has never brought his infidelity up. After counseling, they decided to keep it in the past, but thanks to me, it's being resurrected.

Damian looks at me enraged, and I give him a sheepish smile, which soon turns to a grimace with Sofia's next words, "But hey, at least you didn't fuck my family member, right? Oh, no, wait, you fucking *did*!" she shouts, her face red with anger.

"Fuck's sake, Alexandr, can you not keep it in your fucking pants?" Damian snaps at me to save his hide, and I swallow my chuckle.

Sofia grins. "See, that wasn't so hard, was it, Damian?" I swear her mood swings give me whiplash.

I hear a chuckle from behind. We all turn to see Sergi leaning against the wall with an envelope in his hand and amusement in his eyes. I scowl at him.

"Where have you been? I have fucking things to do, Sergi."

He rolls his eyes at me, then stands straight, walking over to the armchair under the window to my right, and he takes a seat.

"Well, to be fair, Al, your first job is to go get tested, then preferably kill your mistress. Seems she's been going through your phone when you are passed out, getting our account details for our businesses. Three million was transferred to an offshore account; I've just spent an hour getting it all back. And if you're considering going after Phoebe Pie, don't bother; she's already gone," he states, passing us some paperwork but keeping other documents in the envelope.

What the fuck? I look through it, and all the evidence proves what that fucking bitch has been doing. I've been so intent on making Phoebe pay and enjoying the distraction with Candy that I let my guard down. This, right here, is fucking why I'm not Pahkan, and Damian is. I'm a fuckup. I sigh and put my head in my hands. It's a good thing my parents are on a cruise with Sofia's, or I'd be fucking chopped up and fed to the animals I bought Mila, who I am really glad is asleep right now!

Damian sighs. "I can do it if you can't, brother." I snort and shake my head. He's acting like I'm in love with her when, in reality, she was my distraction.

"I'll do it; this is my fault." Then, the last part of what Sergi said comes back, and I stand up.

"What do you mean she's gone? Gone where, and how the fuck would you know?" I growl out.

He sighs. "Sit down, Al; I have a story to tell you all."

I sit reluctantly; he may be my pseudo-brother, but he is also second and higher up than me. He leans his elbows on his knees, linking his hands, with the envelope dangling between them.

"You all know I've been close with Phoebe for years, right?" We all nod. Sofia has made herself comfortable on the biggest armchair in the room, drinking her fruit smoothie. I shake my head. Her pregnancies are crazy.

I look back at Sergi. When I saw her for the first time, I hated how close he and Phoebe were. Every time they would meet up, he wouldn't let us come despite my being engaged to her. Only Mila was allowed to go with him. He'd been meeting up with Phoebe since she was just a small girl, once a month, and would talk to her once a week on the phone.

When they met up, it was the only time we didn't see him for a whole day. Well, until the last five months, that is. He seems to disappear on Sunday mornings and some evenings, but he has yet to tell us where. He will when he's ready.

I sigh. We only met Selene because of the contract, but he never got along with her despite his close friendship with Phoebe.

"Well, when Phoebe left, it devastated me, and when I found out why...." He shakes his head, looks at me, and says, "As with Damian, when he hurt Sofia, I did not kill you because you're my family, and I love you like a brother. You both hurt two women who mean the world to me, who I would die for, but Phoebe, I struggled not to hurt you, Al; she's not just like a little sister to me, she's my blood. " This time, Damian stands up in shock while Sofia's mouth drops open, smoothie dripping down her chin. If his bombshell didn't shock me, I would have laughed. "Juan Garcia is my biological father."

And there is the fucking bomb! He drops his head.

"Why the fuck didn't you tell us? We are your family!" Damian growls out with pain in his voice. I shake my head and look down, hurt that he felt we couldn't be trusted. He sighs again, and I look at him as he looks back at us.

"I've known all my life, Damian; my mother never kept it from me, and your parents and in-laws know, too. I am the rightful heir to the Spanish Mafia, but I don't fucking want it; *he didn't want me!*" I can hear the pain in his voice.

He heaves a heavy breath. "He didn't want me, so I didn't want him! My mother told me about Selene and Phoebe, how they don't know they are related to Juan, and that their father doesn't know. When I was fourteen, my mother thought it would be good to get to know my cousins, but I was dead set against it. I didn't want to know the, but we were all supposed to go to the shooting range together, then to the club. I didn't want to go and meet some spoiled princesses," he growls.

Damian sits back down while I lean forward, giving him my attention. "I was only half right. They introduced me as a family friend, and Selene was eight at the time, already a complete bitch; she would shove Phoebe and pull her hair, cry when she didn't get her own way, and refuse to go anywhere near me. But Phoebe...." A ghost of a smile appears on his lips, and the love of a brother shines through his eyes as he stares ahead, making my eyes water. He got part of a family he always wanted, but jealousy builds in my chest because he spent all that time with her. "She walked right up to me and grabbed hold of my hand while she sucked her thumb. She was only five. Her hair was in pigtails, looking innocent and adorable, and she asked me if I liked chocolate pie, hence her nickname." He chuckles, then looks at us again. "We have been inseparable since. Selene didn't like that I had all her sister's attention, so after a couple of months, her mother stopped bringing her and only brought Phoebe."

I jump in because I have to know. "Did she know then? That you were related?"

He chuckles again and shakes his head. "Not until she came back at sixteen. When she left, we spoke daily on the phone for six years. I'd fly out to see her several times, and you all thought it was a family vacation. Juan knew we were close, and I don't know why, but he decided to tell her that I was her cousin the day she was boarding the plane back home, and made sure to explain how no one knows." He lets out a small laugh, still in the memories. "She confronted me, asked me if it was true, and when I told her yes, she slapped me!" Sofia snorts "Fucking slaps me across the face, threatening me, that if I ever lied to her again, she would disown me, and then she hugged me tight and told me she was glad I was her blood." He smiles.

"I get why you didn't tell us, brother. I wish you had; we could have supported you, but it was your decision. We need to know, though, how did you come across this information on Candy?" Damian questions, and Sergi smiles, handing him the rest of the paperwork in the envelope. I look over to see what it is, and my brows shoot high. "It's the same way I got this information. Phoebe," he replies. I look at him as he continues, "There are three men; she didn't know two of their names, but she knew Grigoriy. The other two are Boris and Leonid. Those are the three who didn't like you taking over. Grigoriy is the frontrunner for finding the young girls or boys in group homes, and the other two pick them up, and then take them to the meeting point for the Mexican Cartel or the Romanians to pick up." Damian curses up a storm while I feel my rage boiling over.

I look at Sergi and ask, "How did you get this out of Phoebe?"

He sighs again.

"I knew she'd be staying at Juan's Mansion in Brooklyn, so I went to talk to her. Well, first, I had a go at her for answering the door without a weapon in her hand; I could have been a serial killer."

Sofia chuckle, "You *are* a serial killer, Serg."

He laughs out loud. "That's what she said," making Sofia smile wide. He looks back at me and says, "Anyway, I knew I'd be the one person she would give the information to; she doesn't like to lie to me, even if she kept quiet about what she'd been learning over the years." I rub my hands down my face, and he continues, "I've assured her we'd sort them out."

Damian nods. "Too fucking right, we will."

I look back at Sergi and ask, "What about Juan? How does he fit into this with you?"

He grunts. "He wants to meet with me, but I don't want anything to do with him. Phoebs told me how his wife Valeria got pissed at him for keeping me a secret for twenty-nine years. Apparently, he wanted nothing to do with me because he was afraid his wife would leave him, but now I'm his only heir. Suddenly, she knows, and he wants contact. She blames him for keeping her child away from her, even though I'm not biologically hers; she doesn't see it that way, but like I told Phoebe, I'm not ready." I nod and get up. He stands, too, and I give him a big hug.

"We'll help you through it, whatever you decide," I whisper, and he nods. Then I turn and go to walk out.

"Where the fuck are you going?" Damian questions, but I continue walking and say over my shoulder, "I have a Don to contact regarding his niece and her whereabouts."

Damian chuckles while Sergi gets a serious look on his face, which makes me pause.

"If she does forgive you, brother, and that is a big *if*, do not hurt her again." I hear the threat, and I'm fucking proud to call him family. I nod, then walk out to my car and go to the office. I'll sort Candy out after I've got my woman back and my ring on her finger. And I'll also tell Mindy where she can go, too.

eleven

Phoebe

I'VE BEEN BACK HOME for about a week now. I'm walking out of my chemistry class when my phone rings. I answer it, trying to juggle my books.

"*Hola, Tio. Cómo estás?*" I ask in Spanish, and he chuckles, loving hearing me talk in his language.

"I'm good, *princesa*; your *tia* has finally let me back in my own bed after months in the guest room." I chuckle. It's not the fact he cheated that one time; she knew about it but decided to move on, and he never did it again. It's the fact she could have been a mother to an amazing man she's, *that's* what she's pissed about. She has it in her head that he would have lived with them. I just don't have the heart to tell her that Sergi would never have left his mother; she was his world and an amazing woman.

Juan snaps me back to him. "Did you see him?" I sigh. I know he wants good news, but Sergi comes first. "I'm sorry, *Tio*, he's just not ready. Twenty-nine years is a long time of hurt and abandonment issues."

He sighs. "I know, sweetheart. Hopefully, he'll talk to me soon, if I keep pursuing it." I smile, and I think they will get along well. Sergi is the spitting image of Juan; how I didn't notice it in the six years I was with him and my grandmother, I honestly don't know.

"Listen, *princesa*, I have another one for you." I stop and move over in the hallway.

"I'm listening, *Tio*." I'm eager to get rid of some more scum. This is what I do, like other assassins trained by the Shadow.

I live to hunt and kill traffickers and rapists.

"A 39-year-old male was inside for child pornography and attempted rape of an 18-year-old. He got out on parole last week for good behavior. A package is being sent to your farm. He has been caught on CCTV raping a 15-year-old girl, and it was brought to my attention. I have investigated him, and he is in contact with the Cartel…and Mihai. It seems Christian was just the front man to hide Mihai's identity."

I suck in a breath. *That cowardly....* I knew I should have just killed the fucker.

"Don't worry, sweetheart, you can go after him once we get this fucker. His name is Thompson Ellison. He's been scoping out the group homes in Casper. All the details will be in the package, but he should be creeping on another group home again tonight."

I growl out, "I'm on it, *Tio*. I'll call once the jobs done."

He chuckles. "My little Angel of Death, don't worry about calling immediately. I know you'll get it done. *Te amo, princesa*." I furrow my brows. I always call him right away, but before I can question him or tell him I love him, too, he hangs up. He actually fucking hangs up. I growl, then walk to my Buick and head home. Abby didn't have classes today, so she will probably be there when the package arrives, putting it in order for me, and making bullet points like always.

Half an hour later, I'm pulling up near the front of the farmhouse. Abby is sitting on the porch with the package already out in organized piles. You've got to love good help from your closest friends. I quickly unbuckle and get out of the car.

"Fuck me, Phoebe, this asshole is sick. I mean, I know there's evil, but the pictures he's saved on his computer from the photos he's taken at the children's home…I can't." She shakes her head.

I frown and have a look, and I'm instantly sickened. Young boys and girls are undressed, and he's even labeled the file as "for later." Yeah, this guy is gone! I storm inside, going through the living area to my bedroom, slamming the door on the wall, and making Ares, who was sunning himself on my windowsill, jump. I stroke his head as an apology and go to change my clothes.

Abby leans against the door frame as I change into my leather pants and crop top, and put on my biker boots. I put my gun behind my back in the slot on the inside of my pants, and grab my knives, placing them in the spaces in my boots. Then, I grab my throwing stars, and they go in the slots on the inside of my top, so I don't cut myself. I made that mistake before. I look at Abby, and she holds out a Kevin's cheeseburger, and I grin. I quickly snatch it and chomp through it before heading toward the kitchen for a bottle of water, and she chuckles.

"Your bike arrived while you were at school." She smirks, and I nod, finishing my burger and taking a few big gulps of water. She gives me a mint, and I thank her and kiss her cheek.

"I should be home by tomorrow, but I'll let you know." She nods and passes me the cliff notes she's made for me. "I know the drill; end the bastard," I smirk, then head out for my bike. I quickly review the notes, spending fifteen minutes studying all the details. It should only take me roughly an hour to get to where I need to go. I place the information in my saddlebag and hop on, before revving my girl and driving off.

It only takes me forty minutes to get to the building the fucker moved into with the help of Mihai, and I look around; there are tall buildings around the group home. I know Thompson lives in the building on the right; he's rented a one-bedroom apartment in the middle so he can get a good view, but likes to go down and sit in his car just to the side of the building, between the left and the one he lives in, to take pictures and help plan the extraction for each child he deems worthy of selling.

I enter the left building, go to the second floor, and enter apartment 2A. It's an apartment my uncle rented under a false name; the information was in the notes Abby gave me. I go to the window and climb out onto the fire escape, then to the rooftop, and set up. I know there are only a few cameras, but I want to avoid getting caught. I take out the very large grappling hook with the rope attached, and secure the hook to the base of the retaining wall at the edge of the roof.

I look at my watch. It's 9 PM. I have roughly two hours before Thompson sneaks down to his car, and I have a perfect view of his driver's side, where, from the angle of the pictures he's taken, I know he sits.

A few minutes later, I hear footsteps from behind me, and I quickly pull out my trusty Glock and point it at the intruder's head. I roll my eyes, and of course, he fucking found me.

"Isn't this the part where you put the gun down, *malen'kaya ptitsa*?"

I snort. "I think I'd rather keep it where it is, thanks. What are you doing here, Alex?" As I talk to him, his eyes take me in, devouring me, and I see them linger on my tattoo. I see his emotions as clear as day crossing his face: sadness, heartbreak, and sorrow when he notices they're sparrows.

I once asked him about the endearment.

"Why, little bird?" I asked, and he looked at me.
"Because you're my sparrow, my joy."
Then he kissed me.

What absolute bullshit! If I were his joy, he wouldn't have fucked my sister.

He looks back at me and says, "I'm here to get my fiancée back." He says it with so much emotion that it almost, *almost* makes me want to give in and go to him, but then I remember what a pig he is, and decide against it. I put my gun back in its spot in the back of my pants, and I turn around to look at the weasel's car.

"Sorry to disappoint, Alex, but that ship sailed long before you got yourself a coke head mistress." I can feel him behind me; he's moved, so his front is nearly touching my back—but not touching, probably knowing I'll break his arm. Or at least try. He *is* third-in-command to a Pahkan, so he's well-trained, too.

I feel his breath against my neck, and I close my eyes. This sucks; I've fucking missed him so much, but he slept with my sister.

"I know I fucked up Phoebs; I only got a mistress to punish you for leaving me; I didn't know you left because of what I did behind closed doors until last week." He tries to pacify me, and I snap. Is he serious? Behind closed doors, really? Is he really trying to downplay the fact that he fucked my fucking sister, and continued to fuck her when I left like it was okay?

I turn around fast—so fast that he takes a step back. I grab a throwing star simultaneously and hold it against his neck. He lifts both of his hands up, but not out of fear. More to prove he won't do anything,

"Behind closed doors? Are you fucking serious?" He swallows, realizing what he said to me. "So you *fuck* my *sister* and some slutty whore, probably for fucking *months*, despite our engagement, and all you can do is label it 'what I did behind closed doors' like you didn't betray me with my *fucking backstabbing sister*!" I shout the last bit, and he takes another step back, eyes wide. Not once in the years we've been together have I ever raised my voice to him. I kept the throwing star raised between us.

"It was the wrong choice of words, Phoebs. I'm sorry, okay, I fucked up, I know—"

I don't let him finish. I twist to my side and sidekick him in the stomach. He grunts in surprise and lands on his ass. I walk toward him and lean over him.

"You disgust me. It was bad enough that a slut was trying to get herself knocked up by you, and you were basically letting her by not using protection, but then you go and fuck my sister, who fucking tried to sell me, even after I fucking left! Then you move a disease-ridden coke head into a hotel and make her your mistress. I don't want you anywhere near me. I might be bound by you, Alexandr, but as far as I'm concerned, you no longer exist. I don't know what you said to my uncle to get him to agree to tell you my whereabouts, and I don't give a fuck. Stay away from me, or next time, you'll learn exactly why I'm called the Angel of Death," I sneer, then turn and walk back to the edge of the building. Looking at this weasel's car again, I ignore the pain I saw in his eyes, but the truth fucking hurts. He did this, not me. We'd be married now, on our way to starting a family like we've always talked about, but he decided to add *extras* he knew I wouldn't be comfortable with. I don't care if he's Bratva, I don't share, and neither does he, so I don't understand why he would think what he was doing was acceptable.

Fucking Juan. Other than Abby, he is the only one who knows where I am; he did this, and I can guarantee he used time with Sergi as a bargaining chip. I swivel around and point my finger at him.

"If I find out that you've used Sergi as a way to get to me, I swear to fucking God, I will castrate you, Alexandr!" He swallows hard, guilt shining in his eyes, and I know he did. I go up to him and punch him in the lip, slitting it, and he takes it, too, knowing he deserves it.

He wipes his lip and grunts. "Sergi agreed; he didn't have to, either, but I know he wants his cousin back home. We all do." I narrow my eyes at him; clearly, Sergi's told them who he is to me. I turn my back on him, go back to the edge of the building again, and lean down, keeping myself hidden while still being able to see the bastard who's going to meet his Maker. I try to hide my guilt for hitting Alex, even though he deserved it for forcing Sergi into a meeting with a man who didn't claim him until it suited him. I love my uncle, but what he did was wrong, and he knows it.

I look at my watch again. 9:55 PM. I sigh. Just over an hour to go. And this is where I stay, at the edge of the building, watching and waiting. I can feel

Alex is still on the roof with me. I can feel his eyes watching me, studying the new me. Well, the new to *him*. I've been this girl since I was ten. I ignore him, and we stay quiet. Then, finally, the sick bastard appears, and I stand, straightening, causing Alex to stand and look over the edge as well.

I smirk. "Well, hello there, darling, it's about time you showed," I sneer evilly. Alex's eyebrows shoot up, and he steps away from me, clearly not used to this Phoebe. I grab my gloves from my pocket and put them on; I don't need any DNA around. Then, I take out my throwing star from my top and examine it. I remove the plastic film that covers it, and Alex's brows furrow.

"*Malen'kaya ptitsa*, I don't think that will work from up here."

I smirk at him, then look at Thompson. I flex my wrist as Alex raises his brows, shocked that I will attempt this. This won't be the first time I've done this; we're only four stories high.

Just as Thompson is about to enter his crappy rust bucket, I throw the star, flexing my wrist at the same time, and it imbeds itself nicely in the side of his neck. I chuckle and look at my ex.

"You were saying?" I look back at the weasel and watch him choke on his own blood while trying to grab the star in the side of his neck.

Five minutes later, he's in a heap on the ground, and I get my burner phone out, dialing my uncle's number. He answers on the second ring.

"Angel," he answers calmly, but I can hear the hesitation.

I sneer, "Job complete, and don't fucking bother calling me for a week, or I'll travel to Spain and make my lovely aunt a widow. You've betrayed me *and* forced Sergi into something he is not ready for in the same night."

He sighs. "Now, sweetheart, I only have your best interest at heart. He—" I hang up on him, then take a loose brick and smash the burner. I pick up the pieces and place them in a plastic bag. I'll burn them once I get home.

I pack up the rest of my stuff, and go to the edge of the building opposite, where there's a dead body. My uncle will have the police out in exactly twenty minutes, just enough time for me to high-tail it out of here. I throw the bag down, and it lands near my bike.

"Phoebe."

I stop short, then turn to look at him and lie through my fucking teeth. "I've moved on, Alex, so it's about time you did, too!" I turn around, grab the rope, and throw it over the wall. I hear him growl loudly, but I ignore him and climb over the wall.

"What are you doing, Phoebs? You can't go down the side of a fucking building."

I continue to ignore him and wrap the rope around my leg to get a tight grip on it before I lean back, hanging off the building.

"Fucking hell, baby, get back over here." He sounds panicked, but tough shit; he's seriously underestimating me. I begin repelling down the building, and I hear Alex shouting at me again, but I continue my descent. A few moments later, I jump the last few feet. I yank the hook hard, and it falls down. I pick it up and put it in my saddle bag, and I climb on the bike, and drive off without looking back.

He is my past; he made sure of that five months ago, and has continued to do so every day since.

twelve

Alexandr

I STAND HERE, staring over the wall as I watch the love of my life fucking climb down the side of the building. When she gets down safely, I breathe a sigh of relief and grab the hook, yanking it from the wall. I put it down and am about to get the rope, so she doesn't get fucking caught, when all of a sudden, it goes over the edge of the building. I look back down, and I see her putting it in her bag, before climbing on her bike—again without a fucking helmet.

She drives off without looking back, and my heart breaks. I feel like I've lost her. Our talk didn't go as planned, which is 100% my fault. I basically tried to bullshit her about sleeping with her own sister, which I continued to do after she left, and I got a mistress as a "fuck you" to her as well. I sigh again and turn to go. I've made sure no cameras are working. I know she has a way to disable them, but I wanted to ensure she was double-protected. I must admit, though, watching her work was the most amazing thing I've seen, and that's saying something, because I helped deliver my nephew.

I return to my rented black Aston Martin and start her up. I know where Phoebe's living, but she needs space tonight. Tomorrow, though, she's mine! So, I'll head to Berry's Inn, where I've booked a room for a few weeks. I'll be showing up at her school tomorrow after her classes; I'm not losing her, not now that I have her in sight again.

Half an hour into the drive back to Mendocino, my phone rings and connects with Bluetooth. I look at the name and sigh.

I answer.

"Juan," I say coldly, and he fucking chuckles.

"Here, I thought you'd be grateful that I told you where my niece lived and what she'd be up to tonight. You are aware that I am actually scared for my life. I trained her, and I know how deadly she is! And I know how much Sergi means to her."

"You're acting like you didn't get anything out of this, Juan, or did I not fucking beg my pseudo-brother to have a meeting with you next month?" I say it with amusement. "You do realize that he and Phoebe are now fucking pissed at me for my involving him, and the only reason why he's agreed is because of your niece and how he wants her happy and at home."

He chuckles again; he is excited to finally meet his estranged son. Sergi was not happy with me after I called him and basically begged him into a meeting with a man who didn't want him growing up. I sigh, feeling like I have betrayed him.

"I don't know what else to do," I admit, and I hear him grunt. He knows his niece better than anyone else.

"You've just got to persevere; you didn't just cheat Alexandr, you took it one step further and slept with her sister over the course of your relationship with Phoebe, then continued to do so even knowing it was the reason she left. If she *does* forgive you, treat her like a queen."

I grunt back, and he hangs up while I sigh again.

Twenty minutes later, I pull up to the inn, only five miles from Phoebe's farm, and head to my room up the stairs. I shake my head, looking around the dull walls, and strip down, heading for a quick shower. I turn the water on and get in despite the cold water, and I sigh. Fuck. I lean my arms against the cold tile wall and tilt my head down, letting the water fall over my head as it heats up. I take a deep breath.

Phoebe comes to mind; fuck, she looks hot in leather. My cock gets hard just at the thought of her, and I reach down. I grip the base and squeeze tight, moving my hand to the tip and continuing the motion. I picture her on her knees in front of me as her tongue pokes out. She slowly licks between the seams of the tip of my cock, lapping up the little bit of cum that drips out, and moans. My hand strokes faster. She takes me into her mouth, and she sucks the tip. I groan as her green eyes stare into mine as she sucks me to the back of her throat, and I come, ropes of my seed spurting out of my body.

I groan, "Phoebe."

I open my eyes, and I see my release going down the drain, making me sigh. No Phoebe, just me.

I quickly wash and get out, drying myself before wrapping the towel around my hips. I wipe the mirror and look to my left pec, where my tattoo from a year ago sits—a sparrow with the letter P in script hanging from its beak. It's got to mean something that she got sparrows, too, right? I still have a chance. She wouldn't have gotten it if I wasn't under her skin, right? I sigh again, then head back into my room and throw the towel on the floor. I grab a pair of boxers, then grab my phone, and sit on the end of my bed. I find Sergi's name and hit dial. It rings about six times before he finally answers, and I furrow my brows.

"Al, is everything okay?"

I look at the time. It's 2:30 AM. I know it's late, but he's usually still out and about, yet he sounds groggy. That's not normal.

"Yeah, I just, uh, Serg, are you okay?"

He clears his throat and chuckles, "I was asleep, Al. It's 2:30 in the morning, brother. How did it go?"

I sigh. He wants to move on from the fact that he is not alert like normal, and it's not even a Sunday.

"It didn't go very well; I might have said some shit about not realizing she knew about the stuff I was doing behind closed doors." The fucker laughs—fucking full-on laughs. I scowl, about to rip him a new one, when suddenly, I hear, "Hmm, babe, what time is it?" and my mouth drops open. Sergi never brings women home; he finds them at the club and fucks them in the corners, but that's it.

What the fuck?

He clears his throat. "It's early, *dragotsennyy*. Go back to sleep, okay?" Then I hear him kiss her, and then some rustling before there's the click of a door, and he clears his throat again.

He called her precious. I think I'm in shock.

"Al, are you still there?" he asks.

He sounds a lot more alert now.

"Sergi, who the fuck was that?"

He sighs. "Not one word to anyone, not Damian, not Phoebe, and certainly not Sofia; those two women will get into my business, and I won't have that, not right now."

I clear my throat. This must be serious. Don't get me wrong, he and I are best friends, but Damian is, more so than me, and Sergi doesn't want him to know. I can understand the women, though.

"As long as it doesn't harm our family, Sergi, you can trust me."

He sighs again. "Her name is Avery Taylor, and she's twenty-three."

I clear my throat again, shocked.

"How'd you meet?" I want to be sure she's not just a spy, but I'm also curious about my long-time friend and brother.

"The Brew Box. She works five evenings a week, which includes all day on Saturdays. She's currently in medical school. She attends New York Medical University but still has eight months left before she graduates and starts her residency at General."

I stay silent for a few minutes, and he lets me process. In all the years we have known him, he has not had a serious relationship.

"It's serious?" I ask, and he grunts out a yes. "Why the secrecy then? You know we have your back, right?" I say softly, hurt that he has kept a lot from us. I understand about his biological father, which is a head fuck, but this?

But then he shocks the shit out of me when he says quietly, "She doesn't know about the Bratva or Mafia world."

"I'm sorry, what?" I sputter, and he quietly chuckles.

"Yeah, imagine going to get a coffee, pissed that another one of your best friends ran away again without a word, so you have a permanent scowl on your face, and you bump into this shy good girl, and she looks at you like you hung the fucking moon. I swear, Al, I felt like someone hit me in the chest when she spoke to me, all quiet and sweet, so I kept going back on the weekdays when I knew I was in the area. And when a customer was giving her grief, I finally stepped in and spoke to her. We started dating like normal couples, and the more we saw each other, the more I fell, and the harder it was to tell her the truth. We spend every Sunday together before I go to Damian's for dinner."

I sigh. "But she doesn't know *you*, Serg." I don't want to hurt him, but he needs to see how bad this will go if she finds out the truth. He lied to her. "Brother, she'll think your relationship is a lie. She will be hurt."

He growls low. "I know, Al, fuck me, do I know. Both you and Damian, you both fucked up. You were worse than him, but both your women ran; he only just managed to convince her to give it another go, and you, well, I'm shocked Phoebe hasn't put a bullet in you yet."

I chuckle at that and decide to give him the distraction he so badly wants.

"No, she just put a throwing star to my throat, then side kicked me in my stomach and sent me flying. All that was after she held her gun to my head." He bursts out in laughter, like the proud cousin he is. I shake my head, refusing to mention the split lip, too; he won't ever let me live it down, even if I did deserve it.

He sobers up and says, "I'll tell her soon. I just want more time; I don't want to lose her, and I guess I'll have to tell Damian as well. He'll be pissed that you knew first." I chuckle again, then quiet down, and I heave a sigh when he comes back to my girl. "She'll come around, Al. Just give her time, keep persevering, and when you get home, you can sort out the women who did you dirty. Mindy and Selene purposely sent her the link; they knew a surprise pregnancy and you being with Selene would make her leave. Even though I'm fairly sure she now knows Mindy was lying, you still fucked her sister. She just needs time. And as for Candy, she's still living it up unaware; she thinks you're out of town on business. She cannot access the businesses, so we don't have to be concerned about her just yet, but I'll keep an eye on her, okay?"

I sigh again. "Thanks, brother."

He chuckles. "Anytime. I'm going back to my woman. Talk soon." He hangs up, and I drop my phone on the bedside table, which automatically starts charging on the charging pad I plugged in. The screen lights up, and a picture of Phoebe studying in the café where we used to meet, pops up. I took it because of how beautiful she looked, practically glowing. I sigh and lay back, closing my eyes, hoping for sleep to come.

I will get you back, baby. You are bound by me, as I am bound by you.

thirteen

Phoebe

I WALK OUT of my laboratory class and bump into a soft body. I look up to see Brent, the weirdo who hasn't stopped asking me out since I arrived. He's about 5'9", has greasy black hair, and a scrawny body covered by a greasy shirt that hangs off his frame. Each time he corners me, I try not to gag on the smell alone. I itch to slice his throat; he has that serial killer vibe. I should know. But I'm the quiet, shy girl, *not* the assassin.

"Excuse me, Brent," I say and try to go around him, but he grabs my arm, making me freeze in shock because he's never actually touched me before. I look up at him to see he's sneering at me.

"I hear you fucked Oliver; your virginity was supposed to be mine!"

What? Okay, so Oliver is a loose end that needs to be tied, and who the hell does this jackass think he is? My virtue and body belong to no one, and how in the hell does he know I'm still a fucking virgin?

"Get your hands off me, Brent, now." I don't correct what Ollie has been saying, I'll be sure to go find him in the cafeteria after this. He fucked with the wrong person. Brent doesn't move his hand, he smirks instead, seeming to think I'm this weak little girl. Well, he's about to get a surprise.

Just as I'm about to grab and break his hand, a strong hand clamps down on it, and I instantly know who it is. My body hums with his presence, always bound by him.

Stupid, traitorous body.

"I believe my fiancée told you to get the fuck off of her." My girlie bits start to tingle, fucking traitorous body, I tell you. For months, I've tried to move on, and nothing, but he speaks all growly, and my body comes alive. It's not fucking fair.

I look up to see Alex's furious face. He towers over Brent at 6'3", and he has his gun in view, which make Brent stiffen when he sees it.

I glare at Alex and mutter, "Ex," making him scowl at me, and I smile sweetly at him.

Because Brent took too long to comply to Alex's command, Alex ripped Brent's hand away, then bent it at an unnatural angle, making me scowl when I hear it crack. Alex smirks at me, obviously reading my mind. Brent starts sobbing, then flees down the empty hallway, making me roll my eyes.

"I wanted to do that!" I whine once he's gone, making Alex chuckle, and then the fucker kisses my head like he used to, making my heart skip a beat.

No, no, I will not fall for it, stupid heart. Stay cold!

He fucked your sister—stay cold!

"I know, *malen'kaya ptitsa*, but I guessed you wanted to keep your *other* persona hidden."

I grumble, knowing he's right, then turn to leave, and Alex follows.

"Where are you off to in such a rush, baby?" I scowl at the nickname, knowing he's used it for the druggy whore.

"I have someone to see in the cafeteria. What are you doing here, Alex? I thought I told you to go, and I'm not your baby; that's your mistress."

He sighs, his face paling a little, but he keeps up with my steps, not missing a beat, as he states, "I'm not giving up on us, Phoebe. I know I fucked up, and honestly, I have no excuse. I just didn't want to pressure you into something you wanted to wait until marriage for. I was trying to...to respect your wishes, I just went about it the wrong way."

He's trying to be sincere, but it's bullshit; if he loved me so much, then he would have waited.

So I stop and look at him and say, as coldly as I can muster without my pain showing, "Yeah, the right way is called using your right-hand, dick, not my sister and your fuck buddies." Then I turn and head into the cafeteria. I stop and look around, still feeling

Alex behind me, when I see Ollie sitting with the jocks, and I smirk. This should be fun.

I stomp over there. I know Alex has waited near the door; he can see I'm in a dangerous mode and clearly wants the entertainment.

I see Abby standing in the buffet line, staring wide-eyed at me as I approach Ollie's table. I come up behind him and use him as a crutch to get on top of the table.

"Phoebe wha—" I don't let the parasite finish; we were okay-ish after his betrayal. I left him alone after he arranged the meeting with the Christian, Damian, and my father despite him lying to me. Well, to be fair, I completely forgot about it, but he's made his own bed with his little stories, putting him back on my radar, and now he can pay.

I place two fingers in my mouth and wolf whistle, getting everyone's attention as they quiet and look at me in confusion. Yeah, I know—not the quiet girl I've been portraying.

I say as timidly as I can, to keep up my persona while internally rolling my eyes, "Excuse me, everyone, I'm not very good at speaking publicly because, obviously, I'm very shy and don't like the attention." I look down, placing my hair behind my ear, keeping up pretenses. I hear Abby and Alex snort, and I just stop short of smirking and rolling my eyes. I look up again, trying to look scared, and state, "I just wanted to let you all know I have not had sexual *anything* with Oliver. I know that's what he's been telling people, and I don't think it's fair that he's lied to everyone about me when I've done nothing but support him and his life choices.

I have video and photographic evidence of him having sexual intercourse with James, the bartender from Kevin's, in the hallway near the men's bathrooms. It's how I found out he was cheating on me." I hear everyone gasp while Oliver sucks in a sharp breath. I fake a sniffle and wipe under my right eye with the back of my hand like I'm upset. "I just wanted you all to know. Thank you." Then I get down, again by using Ollie, who's gone completely still as everyone whispers about him. His friends at the table are staring at him in shock, and I lean down, trying to look sympathetic toward him and sorry for ratting him out and whisper, "What I did in that hallway will be child's play to what I'll do to you if you don't pack your shit and leave this town. You had the balls to try and steal from me, so go steal from your family, take James and leave, or you're dead. Don't believe me, ask Christian. Oh no, wait, you can't, because I shot him in the head right after I killed four of his men." He pales and swallows hard.

I then wave to Abby, who is trying hard to hide her laughter, and walk back to Alex, whose grinning. Fuck, he is not going to leave, is he? I sigh.

When I get closer, knowing his help might keep me alive, I state lowly, "You and I need to talk about Mihai. Seems as though you don't want to listen to me and fuck off, so I'll tell you he's still trafficking." The amusement he had on his face disappears, and the cold-blooded killer resurfaces. He nods, then follows me toward the parking area, keeping his distance.

Once we get to my Buick, I turn toward him and ask, "You know where I live?" I know he does, but I wanted to make sure. He nods, and I roll my eyes, causing him to chuckle. I open my car door and climb in, but before I shut the door again, I say, "See you in thirty."

He closes the door for me, then walks over to his black Aston Martin while I put my car into gear and head toward my farm, knowing Abby is going over some guy's place tonight. I pray Goosy is there when I get home. I could use a laugh.

Halfway home, I look in my mirror and see Alex behind me, and my heart aches. Every time he's near, my cold mask slips a little. A lone tear slips down my cheek, and I quickly wipe it away, then focus on the road. There's just no coming back from the pain he caused.

Fifteen minutes later, we arrive at my farm, and I smirk. Goosy is on the steps, antagonizing Ares again, giving me the laugh I desperately wanted.

I get out of my car before I put my hands on my hips, biting my bottom lip, trying to contain my laughter. Goosy is flapping his wings at the window, while Ares is scratching at the glass, hissing. I shake my head as Alex approaches me, touching my hip. His touch warms me, making my traitorous body tingle all over as he leans down and growls low in my ear, making my girlie bits tingle, too.

"Do me a favor, *malen'kaya ptitsa*, get that goose away from Ares before I shoot the fucker."

I snort. I swear he fucking loves my cat more than he loves his cock. I go to take a step away from him, but he holds me tighter and states, "Five seconds, Phoebs, and the bird is dead."

I lost it. I couldn't control my laughter even if I tried.

He scowls at me before he starts to count down, reaching for his gun and making my eyes widen, realizing he means it.

"Five, four, three…." He thumbs off the safety, and I leg it toward Goosy, and shoo him away from the window, knowing I don't have time for a sneaky grab with him even though his life depends on it. He moves, flapping his wings, unhappy about being shooed away, and heads toward the pond.

I turn and look at Alex, putting my hands on my hips, and scowling at him, but he smirks at me, then heads toward the front door and opens it, where he's met by his friend, the traitor. Ares meows up at him, going in between his legs, making Alex bend down and pick the little traitor up.

To my cat, he coos, "I knew she'd keep you. I missed you, buddy. Did you miss me?" all while scratching behind his ear. I burst out in laughter; I can't help it. A big, badass Bratva *brigadier* was cooing to a cat—a freaking cat. I have literal tears in my eyes.

"You quite done, *malen'kaya ptitsa?*" he asks sarcastically, making me look up at him and lose it again when I see Ares lying across the back of his shoulders. He shakes his head, then heads further inside the house with my little traitor, leaving me to calm down.

It takes me several minutes before I go inside my house. As I walk through the open-plan living area, I notice him at the breakfast counter with a cup of coffee, making me scowl until I see he's made my vanilla latte, and my mouth begins to water. He always did make the best lattes, so I'll let him off this once. I sit on the other side of the counter, pick up my drink, and take a sip, humming to myself. He may be a pig, but damn, can the man make a good latte. He clears his throat, and I look up to see him smiling at me, and I shake my head.

"This isn't like a few years ago, Alex. You can't make me my drink, and then I'll say we'll be friends again."

He gives me a sad smile and states, "Good, because I don't want to be in the friendzone, Phoebe, I want my woman back."

I look at him, shocked. How can he possibly think I'd take him back?

He raises his hands when he notices my expression and says, "I know I fucked up. I know I have a lot of work ahead of me, but you're bound by me, Phoebe. You know you are, and you always have been. I have to live with my fuckup every day, and I know I should never have gotten a fucking mistress." He sighs, and I look away until he says his next words, "Christian said you were no longer pure."

I snort. What a fucking hypocrite, and oh, how wrong he is, but I'm not going to correct him; it's none of his fucking business. Plus, it'll only make his ego even bigger than it already is.

He rolls his eyes at me. "I made it okay, in my head, that I had Candy and still would have had Candy as your punishment when I got you back, because you slept with someone else. I know I don't have a leg to stand on. I know I'm the biggest fucking hypocrite going."

I sigh. "I don't want to talk about this, Alexandr. You're here so we can discuss the Romanians, not *us* or what you did, because it's all in the past, including our engagement."

He gets up, placing Ares on his cat tree in the corner of the dining area, then walks toward me, before he starts to pace. I sit here, watching him go back and forth, and as I am about to ask him to sit his ass down so we can discuss a plan to get rid of Mihai, who I should have just fucking killed but didn't because I thought he had no clue what his so-called boss was doing, he starts to talk, shocking me speechless.

fourteen

Alexandr

I PACE in front of her.

I know she doesn't want to discuss us, but I won't let her give up on our future just yet. I know I'm a hypocrite, but I love her, I have for a long time, and I can't lose her.

I stop in front of her and heave out a heavy breath, hoping this goes my way.

"I know you don't want to talk about it, and I know you believe there isn't an us, but there is because you're bound to me. Phoebe, you and I—we're connected. I didn't go about things the right way, I know this. I should have learned from my brother's mistakes, but I didn't. He even tried talking to me, and I ignored him. I have no one to blame but myself. I can't let you go, *malen'kaya ptitsa.*"

She looks down at her lap, but I continue, "One year." Her head snaps up—so fast, I think she may have given herself whiplash.

She asks, "What?"

I smile and reach out, tucking her hair behind her ear, loving the pink in it. I can see the conflict in her eyes; she wants my touch, but the hurt I gave her outweighs her feelings for me. "Give me one year." She shakes her head. "Just hear me out, please. "I know I don't deserve to plead, but please, Phoebs, hear me out." She sighs, and as I'm about to talk, I hear a female voice behind me.

"This should be good."

I growl, knowing it's her roommate, Abby. My background research showed how close they've become, so I know I can't kill her for interrupting. Phoebe's scowl confirms my thought. She turns her attention to her friend.

"What happened to Luke, or was it Tim?" my girl asks, making Abby chuckle.

"It's Anthony this time, and he's waiting for me outside. I forgot to grab my purse this morning. Are you good?" I see her cock her head in my direction, and then Phoebe sighs and nods. Abby gives her a small smile, then a side hug and a kiss on the cheek. She then looks at me, her multi-colored hair in a messy bun, and dark brown eyes assessing me. "I know what you were just about to suggest. If she goes for it and you hurt her again, I will skin you alive. Our girl taught me most of what she knows, got it!" Both my eyebrows shoot to my hairline.

I nod and give her a smile, while Phoebe chuckles at her friend's threat.

"Wish me luck for a good orgasm," Abby chuckles as she goes out the front door.

I look at Phoebe, my eyes saying *"really?"*, and all she does is shrug as she blushes. I chuckle, and she narrows her eyes at me. So, placing my hands up in a surrender motion, I continue what I was going to say.

"Give me one year to prove I won't hurt you, one year to convince you to come home and transfer vet schools, one year to prove all I want and need is you. And, if in a year, you realize how much we belong together, then we get married and finally start the family we've always talked about." I hold my breath. I only thought of this in the car; it would mean I'd have to travel back and forth several times from here to New York, but I know my brother would understand.

She taps her finger on the counter, and stares at the wall for about five minutes, before she finally looks up at me.

"What happens if you fail?" she inquires coldly.

My heart is in my throat, and I clear it to eliminate the lump. "Then I will never contact you again. I'll allow you to move on, and I'll ensure your father and sister, if you haven't killed her yet, leave you alone, too."

She smirks about murdering her sister, then she sighs, gets up, and goes down the hallway to the right. I stand here for ten minutes, letting her have her time before I finally give in and find her. As I go down the hallway, I notice a door open at the end, and go through it. She's sitting in the middle of her bed, pictures of us are in front of her, and my heart hurts for what I've done. I watched my brother do the same thing, and instead of learning from his mistakes, I followed in his footsteps.

I step in her room and look around. It doesn't seem like hers; one wall is dark gray, and the rest is light, with dark gray curtains. She has a double door to what I'm guessing is her walk-in closet, and another door that leads to a bathroom. She has a king-sized bed with gray sheets, where Ares has made himself comfy on her pillow. I walk over to her, sit on the edge of the bed beside her, and look at the pictures. There must be over twenty of them from our time together. From banquets to just us goofing around at the café, I smile sadly; I've fucking missed her. Candy was really just a distraction. I'm a dickhead for thinking I could use her to punish my girl for *my* fucking mistakes.

I wait patiently for her to talk, and when she does, it's not what I want to talk about, but I placate her for now.

"We need to kill Mihai, or *I* need to, but I'd need the Bratva, and the Greeks and Italians as backup. I have the proof, so the council shouldn't be too upset, especially since he's been the Romanian boss all along, using Christian as the fall guy."

I clear my throat. "I've already sent a message to Damian; he will set up a meeting at Volkov & Co. in two days. You are welcome to come. I wasn't aware of Christian, so I'll let Damian know." She nods and goes quiet again, and I let her. This is how she processes things.

I pick up one of the pictures, and I smile. It was my birthday last year, and she shoved the cake into my face. In the picture, I'm looking at her in shock while her hands are covered in cake in front of her face, which is lifted back, laughing. Sergi caught it on camera.

I chuckle quietly but tense when she finally says, "I loved you."

I suck in a breath but stay quiet while she stares at the pictures. "I didn't want to, but I fell hard; I dropped my mask for you and became the girl I used to be before I became *this* person." She motions to herself with her hand as a lone tear falls from her eye. I gently wipe it away, cupping her cheek, hoping she doesn't push me away, even though I deserve it. She leans into my touch instead, and my eyes water as she looks at me, and finally, she shows me her vulnerability.

The pain in her eyes is unbearable, and I have to fight not to look away.

"I was bound by you when I shouldn't have been; you were supposed to be my sister's, and I fell for you when I didn't want to, and you destroyed me to the point where I placed the cold-killer mask on permanently. You swore you wouldn't do what Damian had done to Sofia." She sniffles, and my heart breaks at what I have done.

"How do you expect me to give you a year when you did what you did?" I close my eyes, squeezing them tight, as she continues, "We're not just talking about some random women here, Alex, we're talking about my sister, the girl who tried to sell me for her own gain. My blood."

I look at her, and I know what I have to do. Nothing I say will convince her; I'm the villain in her story, but I know someone who will help her make sense of her thoughts. I lean forward and place a gentle kiss on her forehead, and I whisper, "I love you, *malen'kaya ptitsa*, I just didn't show it how I should have. What I did was inexcusable, and something you should punish me for every day for the rest of our lives. I know nothing I say will convince you, so what I'm going to do is go into your kitchen, and I'm going to make you your favorite baked moussaka, even though I hate it." I chuckle a little, and a sad smile appears on her face. "And I'm going to leave my phone with you."

I kiss her forehead again and get up, missing her body heat next to mine, but instead of returning to her, I get my phone out of my jeans and hand it to her. "The code is your birthday. Call Sofia."

More tears fall from her eyes when she realizes what I'm doing—giving her time to process the offer but, more importantly, helping her contact a woman she became close to before she left—the same woman who also ran because of a Volkov.

I give her a small smile, turn, and leave her room, heading for the kitchen with Ares on at heels. I place my palms on the edge of the sink, hang my head, and take a deep breath, hoping and praying she accepts the offer, and that Sofia can help. If that doesn't work, I've got one last ace up my sleeve, a woman Phoebe adores....

My mama!

fifteen

Phoebe

I STARE at his phone for a little while. I have remained strong for months, but when he enters my life, and my armor starts to melt, I feel freaking weak, especially when it is him. He's my heart.

But he broke it.

I pick up his phone and see his lock screen picture, and a tear leaks out. It's me at the Precious café, head down, doing my schoolwork. I quickly wipe the tears and unlock his phone, and, as another picture greets my eyes, more tears fall. We're smiling at the camera outside a concert he took me to early last year. I have pink glitter all over my hair and a massive smile, while he's holding me tightly, with a smile just as big.

Was it all a lie?

He looked happy, yet he was sleeping with my sister, so he couldn't have been.

I wipe the tears again and find Sofia's number, ignoring his messages that keep popping up, refusing to see if it's a woman. I press CALL.

It rings a couple of times before my friend, whom I've missed dearly, answers.

"Al, please tell me you've managed to fix your stupid ass fuck up and bring my daughter's favorite person home, because, if not, I'm going to kick your ass." I bite my lip to stop my laughter, before I hear Damian in the background say, "*Malyshka*, don't go threatening to kick my brother's ass; you're pregnant, so I'll kick it instead."

I lose it and burst out in laughter, causing Sofia to gasp.

"Phoebe?"

I clear my throat. "Yeah, it's me."

I hear her sniffle, and another tear falls down my cheek, hating that I've upset her. I didn't realize she was having another baby, though I've been keeping up with her kids. Maksim is only roughly five months old.

Damian doesn't wait around before snatching the phone.

I hear a rustle at the end before he speaks, "Alexandr, what the fuck did you say to make my wife cry?" he growls, and I giggle.

"Sorry, Damian, not Alex."

I hear him sigh in relief, and then say, "I'll go get her ice cream." My mouth drops open, jealous that she gets ice cream like our usual routine for girl chats, and I don't, because I haven't been to the store. I pout until the door to my room opens, and Alex comes in with some chocolate and vanilla ice cream. My tears fall again.

Fuck sake, where's my kill-bitch exterior gone?

Alex smiles and leans down before he wipes the tears away, then hands me the tub with a spoon, kisses my forehead again, and leaves. I hear Sofia chuckle when I sniffle.

"I'm guessing a certain brother-in-law gave you ice cream, too."

I chuckle. "Of course, he did; the men know we like to talk while drunk on creamy goodness, although I didn't even have any in the freezer, so God knows how he got it here."

She chuckles. "How are you, friend?" she asks softly, and my dam breaks for the first time since I left. I burst into tears, sobs wracking from my body, my heartbreak screaming from my body.

I hear Sofia sniffle. "Let it all out, darling."

And I do.

I can hear Alex on the other side of my door, and I think he banged his head on it in frustration, but I can't be sure. My whole body shakes with sobs as I cry uncontrollably, all while Sofia tries to soothe me. When I finally calm down, she brings out my laughter.

"Well, despite the Angel of Death title and the stone-cold bitch face you've had these days, at least you didn't wait three years to have your breakdown." She laughs with me.

I'm quiet for a moment, before I finally talk to my friend, someone who knows what it feels like to be destroyed by a Volkov.

"I don't know what to do," I whisper. "He wants me to give him a year, but I don't think I can do it, but I know I'm bound by him, too. He hurt me badly, so how can I go against my beliefs and not look like an idiot for even thinking of giving it a chance again after what he's done?" A small sob escapes.

She whispers, "I know what he did was a complete fuckup, believe me, I know more than others. I struggled with what Damian did, and I didn't want to try again because of my pride and my heart, too."

I sniffle again and stab my ice cream. "Then how did you do it? How did you learn to forgive him? Was it because of Mila?" I have always wondered how she could take him back after what he did—I mean, seriously, he slept with her cousin.

She sighs. "I've always loved Damian, even when I shouldn't have. He was and is my best friend. When he found me, I was adamant he would only have access to Mila; he hurt me severely, but so did the rest of my family. It took everything I am, plus the encouragement of Adam, Bruce, and April to even give Damian a chance. Then there was the counseling."

I sniffle again as I take in some more ice cream goodness.

"I don't think counseling would work for us, Sof."

I hear her sigh, and then moan over the ice cream, causing me to giggle.

"I know it won't, but let me ask you a question." I clear my throat and wait. "Forget the badass bitch you have become, forget your family and mine, and go back to that quiet, shy girl you once were, and think. Think about how you would feel if you lost him tomorrow, how would you feel if he settled down with another, how would you feel if he made a family with someone else." My breathing picks up, a hollow feeling in the pit of my stomach intensifies the more she speaks, and more tears fall.

"You love him. You love him with everything that you are. It's not about the other women; you'd kick his ass and shove his balls down his throat for sleeping with others behind your back, because he thought it was out of duty for your honor not to pressure you. Fucking men, I swear they're stupid." I giggle because she's not wrong; I still need to smack him, too, because that split lip was for Sergi. "It's the fact he slept with your sister, your blood family, who has been trying to sell you to pay off her debts, that is what's holding you back."

I sniffle again. "How can I look past something like that?"

She chuckles evilly, making my brows furrow, then I hear Damian in the background say, "Fuck, I'm hiding the guns."

I burst out in laughter.

"Well, darling, you make him suffer, of course. Think about it, Phoebs, one year without him getting laid." My mouth opens in an "ah ha" moment.

"All jokes aside, you need to figure out if losing him permanently and him making that coke-head bitch his actual wife, outweighs all the negatives you feel. Giving him a shot at trying for a year may be your one last shot at having your happily ever after."

I sigh and look out my bedroom window. I cannot wait to get some horses and goats grazing in the distance.

"Tell me how my niece is doing; I miss her, and how is my nephew? Is he chubby? Chubby babies are always the best, and couldn't Damian wait at least a year before knocking you up again?" She bursts out in laughter, and we spend over an hour on the phone, catching up.

I missed her.

After we hang up and all the ice cream is gone, I stare at the wall for about five minutes, my mind going over everything. When my phone beeps, I look at it to see a message from Sergi, and I smile. I open it, and I laugh *and* cry.

> Sergi: have courage, be brave, and think with your heart. If he hurts you again, I'll skin him alive for you.

I sigh, knowing what I have to do. I'll regret it if I don't, but I may also regret it if I do.

As I walk into the kitchen, I see he's dishing up the baked moussaka with a side salad, and I smile a little. Since my grandmother died, he's the only one who has managed to bake it perfectly. He looks up as I walk in and gives me a sad smile. I can see the pain in his eyes, and it confirms he heard my breakdown. I go over to him, his eyes pinned to mine, and when I'm close, I ram my knee into his balls. He cups them, then falls to the floor.

Coughing, he says, "Yep, I definitely deserved that, but fuck, sweetheart, don't you want any kids?"

I smirk, happy with the endearment change, and take a picture of him kneeling on the floor, his head down, one hand on his junk, the other placed flat on the floor to keep him upright. I send the photo to Sofia, Sergi, and Abby. Then I go and get my plate, sit at the dining table that he's set up, and start to eat the goodness he's cooked me. My phone beeps three times.

> Abby: fuck yes, girl! By the way, I do think you need to consider his offer. I know what he did was fucking shitty, but you're not happy, Hun. I love you.

I smile a sad smile, knowing she's right. I look at the other two messages and burst out in laughter.

> Sergi: fuck Phoebe Pie; you might need them one day.

> Sofia: oh my fucking God, that's what I'm talking about. Why the fuck didn't I think to do that to Damian?

"Seriously, Phoeb, you sent a picture to Sofia? Damian's going to be fucking pissed at me now; you're giving her ideas," he growls out from the floor, looking at my phone in my hand.

I look at him and flutter my, and smile sweetly. "And Abby and Sergi."

He shakes his head and gingerly gets up, grabbing his plate, before he sits next to me at the table. He groans a little, making me giggle, then places his hand on my knee, like he used to, and starts to eat. I sigh and continue eating in silence because, seriously, this is fucking delicious.

Once we're finished, he looks at me, and I finally speak, "Sofia is right, it's not about the fact you were a pig, it doesn't matter how many excuses you gave yourself; you knew my stand on infidelity, you knew I didn't give a fuck about other Bratva men having mistresses, I cared about you. A marriage where the husband screwed around is something I never wanted for myself; it was against my beliefs, and you went against what is at the core of me. That's why I kneed you in the balls." I take a deep breath. "It's the fact you slept with my sister that I'm struggling with."

His eyes turn sad.

"I don't know how to move past it, Alex. How do I try for a year, when all I see is you with her? Heck, one of the women you slept with accused you of getting her pregnant."

He sighs and runs his hand through his hair. "She's not pregnant, she was bullshitting. Damian and I took her to our doctor for the shot each year, and when we saw the link and her accusations, the doctor gave her an ultrasound, and there was no baby." I look down, and he places two fingers under my chin. "I know it's fucked up. Us Volkov men, we're not very smart." I give a small smile, and he continues, rubbing his thumb on my jaw. "I know I can't take back what I did with the other women or Selene, and I know you don't want to hear this, but I never fucked her cunt, never, always her mouth or ass." I squeeze my eyes shut; he's right, I didn't want to hear that. He puts a little pressure on my jaw, and I open my eyes, which have turned wet.

He whispers, "I know I can't turn back time, I know this is something you're going to struggle with and most likely throw back in my face when we have arguments, but I'm willing to try because I can't live without you anymore."

A tear leaks down my cheek, and he wipes it away.

"I love you, Phoebe. Do I hate that you've slept with someone else? Fuck yes, but I'm choosing to look past it because of how shitty I've been to you. I deserve the punishment of knowing someone else touched what was mine."

I suck in a breath; he still thinks I've slept with someone else.

I clear my throat about to tell him the truth when he talks again, "I want to try again. There are no other people involved, just you and me. I'll travel back and forth, so you don't have to leave here. I'll put a tracker on my phone so that. when I'm not with you, you can see where I am at all times. I'll keep you updated until you can learn to trust me again. Please, sweetheart, don't make me call my mother, because I will. I don't care that she's on a cruise." I giggle, then sniffle, before he leans his forehead against mine, and I sigh, hoping I don't regret my decision.

I nod, and he smiles brightly, and presses his lips gently to mine.

I feel like I'm home.

Which is a scary thought after everything he has done.

sixteen

Alexandr – One Month Later

I KEEP PACING back and forth,

"Al, will you sit the fuck down?" Sergi snaps; he hates it when I pace, but not telling his woman the truth about who he is is starting to get to him. I raise a brow at him, and he sighs while Damian chuckles.

"She'll be here any minute."

I sigh, knowing he's right, but don't sit down; we're in the conference room at Volkov & Co. about to have a meeting where we'll present the proof of Mihai trafficking underage children, the scumbag. About a week after Phoebe decided to give me a chance, we met with Damian and Juan on a conference call, and we agreed to monitor Mihai, and get proof, before we strike, but keep intercepting the children.

We live by a code. For centuries, one man, a previous Don—in honor of each Familia, and a previous Pahkan—in honor of the Bratva, group together as a council. They ensure heads of each family stick to certain rules. Embezzlement from your own men is one of the sins against the code, and an act of treason, if committed, that will be dealt with by death. That's what Phoebe did with Christian. Another broken code is poaching another's territory or selling their own product on another's territory, which is what Mihai is currently trying to do to keep the Feds off of his back. If caught, it'll look like one of *us* is into human trafficking.

Today, we're meeting with them and the heads of the Irish and Greek families, but we haven't sent an invitation to Mihai.

The door opens, and the three elders enter. I see my father instantly, as well as Stefano, and an elder from the Irish, Liam, who're all previous heads of the families. My father comes up to me and gives me a hug, while Stefano slaps me on the back, before he goes to take a seat.

My father looks at me with concern. "How are things?"

I sigh. He and mother were excited about Phoebe's willingness to give me a year. My mother thinks the Volkov charm will work again, well, she is praying it does, or apparently, she's disowning me; Phoebe's another daughter to her.

"As good as can be…she's trying."

He nods, giving me a sad smile, then takes a seat. I wasn't lying; she has been trying, though we haven't done more than a peck, she lets me hold her hand now, even though it took two weeks for her to. She's talking to me more now as well, telling me about school and her life. Apparently, after I broke that Brent guy's hand, he transferred schools. She had a twinkle in her eye when she explained. It is like we were *us* again.

Baby steps.

The door opens again, and Noah walks in with Basil behind them. Noah nods at me, slapping a hand on my shoulder, and greets Damian, while Basil comes to me and says, "How's my daughter?"

I nod. "She's doing okay."

He sighs and nods, then takes a seat. She's still refusing to sit down with him, and he's disappointed, but it's expected; he hasn't exactly been a father to her. As it stands, Selene can do no wrong in his eyes despite her trying to sell his other daughter. He was supposed to monitor her, but I don't think he is, which pisses me off even more; he's blind, and Phoebe doesn't want anything to do with him anymore.

Each man in the room has two men with them; one stands behind their family head, while the other sits beside him.

The door finally opens again, and I smile my first smile all day as my girl walks through, looking badass in her leather, showing us that the Angel of Death is present.

Just when I thought she'd ignore me because she's donned her mask, she doesn't. She walks up to me and places a peck on my lips. I smile again and squeeze her hip. She gives me a wink, then sits next to Sergi, who will be acting as her guard today while I'll act as Damian's. We didn't bring anyone else because our building was full of our men, and about eight men line the walls inside the room. I fought Phoebe about her sitting next to Sergi. I wanted to be with her, but she stated it would make her look weak, so I folded this once.

I sit next to Damian as Sergi sits on his other side, with Phoebe next to him.

All eyes turn toward my brother, and I smirk. They all think he's taking charge of the meeting, but he is not; this is Phoebe's show. Damian smirks, too, and while I hear Sergi chuckle quietly, all the men around the table frown, looking at each other, confused.

Damian stands to get the meeting started. "Okay, gentlemen, let's start this meeting, shall we?"

A man who came with Noah clears his throat and questions, "Where's Mihai?"

Damian looks at him and says, "Unfortunately, Patrick, Mihai will not be joining us; not only do the Romanians not care about keeping the peace in these meetings, but it is about him." He looks at each man, and they nod in silent agreement. Patrick bowed his head slightly out of respect; he'd spoken out of turn, making Noah look weak. Noah scowls at his man and swirls his finger, telling his men to swap positions. Patrick pales slightly while doing so.

Damian continues as he looks at my woman. "The floor is all yours." He smirks.

Her face doesn't change, keeping in character, but her eyes show amusement toward my brother. He, Sergi, and I have to hold in our chuckles, shit's about to get funny.

She stands and looks around the men. The men who are not family heads frown; only Stefano and my father look at her with pride, while Basil sits in confusion about why she's taking charge.

"Gentleman, I would like to thank you all for coming. I understand how busy you are. There is one additional person who would like to be involved, so I'll patch him through. I will be representing him in person while he listens in."

She gets her phone and dials her uncle while the men frown again, and just as Juan answers the phone, without so much as a hello, the man seated next to Basil speaks up.

Shit, it's about to get bloody. I rub my hands together. Daddy's getting Ares his new bed tonight.

"Really, Damian, letting a little girl playing dress up take over our meeting? What the fuck is this? Women know their place; it's at home cleaning and popping out babies, not getting in our fucking business," he says, looking at Basil. "What is your daughter doing, *Nonos*? This is an embarrassment to our council." He growls the last bit as Phoebe sits down.

I hear a slight chuckle from the phone line, and I have to bite my tongue, wanting to kill the fucker for speaking about her like that, but I keep my mouth shut. I don't want her to think that I don't believe in her, and plus, she's now got her knife out, twisting it in her fingers. She's already hurt my balls, and I don't fancy getting stabbed as well.

I look at my brother and Sergi, and they're both smirking. I shake my head.

"You have a problem with me being here, Belen? Because I'm quite sure you didn't have a problem fucking Selene's ass over our dining table when you thought the house was empty last year." She says it coldly, and Basil's amusement turns to venom while Belen stills, then quickly snaps out of it.

"You're a lying whore. You're the one who fucked your father's men behind his back; you shouldn't even fucking be in this room, bitch."

The men at our table grow extremely silent; half don't know what to say, while my father is being held down by Stefano. You don't insult a woman who he sees as his daughter. I look at Sergi and see that Phoebe is also trying to keep him in place.

I look at Basil, and he seems, by the glares he's sending his daughter, like he believes his guard, and that has my rage boiling. Damian has to put a hand on my shoulder to keep me in place. And Basil fucking wonders why his daughter wants fuck all to do with him. I can also see Stefano fuming, but he is trying to keep it under wraps to keep control of my father.

Juan chuckles. "I really wish I was there now because this just got entertaining."

All the men looked at the phone, confused; they recognized his voice but couldn't understand why my girl had contact with him.

She smiles sweetly. "Gentlemen, I believe you all know my uncle, Godfather of the Spanish Mafia, Juan Garcia." Belen doesn't seem deterred by the recent news. I know he wasn't there when she killed Christian, so he's just fucking ignorant.

"I don't give a shit who your uncle is. Your whore ass shouldn't be here; what you did to your sister is despicable; you even got your father to ignore her for months. Your're pathetic."

I growl, ready to jump from my seat, but Phoebe just laughs. "You mean the sister who has you completely fooled? The one who tried to sell me to Christian because she owed him thousands in drug money? The same one who likes to eat pussy while my so-called fiancé is busy fucking the girl who's trying to get my sister off. That sister?"

Belen just laughs. "You're bullshitting yet again, so your father cuts her off. You're a spiteful bitch, and you're a traitor; leaving your contract marriage to Alexandr is punishable by death. A coward is what you are."

It happens fast, so fast that we all look in shock. Phoebe is out of her seat in seconds. She jumps on top of the table and slides down toward Belen, before she stabs her knife into his hand. He screams out while I shoot up from my seat and raise my hand, making the men look at me, ready to get their guns out, thinking that is what I'm doing until I shout, "Called it!"

Damian and Sergi groan out loud while I grin like a loon; they thought she'd keep her cool. They each retrieved $400 from their pockets, and pass it over to me, and I smirk. The men in the room all raise their brows in confusion while Juan chuckles over the line.

"How much did you win, Alex?"

I state, "$800," with a grin.

I look at Phoebe, and she rolls her eyes.

"Can we get back to it, please?" she asks sarcastically.

I chuckle. "You won't be rolling your eyes when I get that new cat bed for Ares you said wasn't worth the money. Now, because Damian and Sergi lost the bet, he can have it." Both men scowl while Phoebe chuckles, then turns back to Belen, who has gone pale. Her father looks at her in disgust, still believing his man, and I sigh; he has no chance of a meeting now.

Phoebe starts to talk again, gaining my full attention.

"Tell me something, Belen. What did dear old Daddy say about what happened to Christian?" Basil stills, his eyes closing slowly, while Belen stutters out in pain, "T-that a s-stray b-bullet h-hit him."

She chuckles, then leans down close. "Wrong, I killed him. I shot him between the eyes."

He chuckles darkly despite the knife in his hand. "Yeah, right, you're nothing but a weak bitch. This here is b-because d-daddy is watching."

She tsks at him. "Ever hear of the Shadow."

His brow furrows. "Everyone has, y-you stupid b-bitch."

"Did you know that she was my grandmother?" He pales and shakes his head, not believing it. She leans down and whispers, just loud enough that we can all still hear, "Have you ever heard of the Angel of Death?" He looks ready to pass out, and not from the blood loss.

"N-no, you're not her, y-you're weak, a-and s-shy."

She smiles her evil smile, making Noah, Liam, and their men all look at her in shock, and grow pale, including some of ours who were unaware of Phoebe's lifestyle.

"Actually, Belen, I am; my grandmother and my *tio* Juan taught me to be the best of the best assassins going and, not to brag or anything, but I am."

She pulls the knife from his hand.

seventeen

Phoebe

THIS MONTH HAS BEEN DIFFICULT; trying to give Alex a real chance without wanting to smack him several times is hard. He's at my house Monday through Wednesday, then Thursday night until Saturday morning, meaning he only goes home to New York on Thursday mornings, and all say Sunday. He meets me at school, cooks me dinner, and puts me first, and I didn't realize exactly how much I'd missed him until he was back in my life; then he had to leave for New York again. My heart, body, and soul are bound by him; they have been since I was nineteen, and it's hard because one minute we'll be having a laugh, then the next, pictures of him and other women will pop into my head.

I know it's only been a month, but I don't know if I can forgive and forget. Too much water may have flowed under the bridge.

Currently, I'm in this meeting being judged by all the men because I'm female, but the shit Belen just spewed my way has pissed me off. My fucking father, who has been trying to get a meeting with me this past month, believes every word he said because, apparently, the only thing my sister did wrong was trying to sell me for her own selfish needs, and my father believes every lie she told him. According to Alex, my father stated Selene was in a bad place and didn't want to disappoint him, so with him sitting there judging me, I snapped.

Oh well, at least Ares gets the ridiculous bed now.

I'm brought back to the meeting when my father snaps, "Phoebe, you can't just stab one of my men for stating the truth about you. Selene has already told us everything you've done over the years. I know that's my fault for neglecting you and trying to protect you, but this is not okay; he is my man, and this is a punishment worth discussing with the council." I shake my head as Belen smirks at me. I smirk back, making his falter, and he starts to pale when he notices how cold my eyes have gone, realizing I'm the biggest threat in the room and he underestimated me.

I take my knife and slice his throat from ear to ear, and blood spurts out over the table while my father stands and shouts, "For fuck's sake, Phoebe, you're not stable!"

I look at him with my cold eyes, making him pause when he notices his daughter is gone, and the killer is in place.

As coldly as possible, I say, "Belen took a 5-year-old girl out of the group home on 2nd last night, and dropped her off in a residential home in your territory. One of Mihai's men was there to pick her up. I retrieved the child, placed her in a safe house with a new family, gutted the man who was at the collection point, and sent his remains to Mihai. You're welcome, Father. Oh, and of course, I'm not stable; I'm the best fucking assassin the Mafia and Bratva have seen." My father pales, and he's about to open his mouth, most likely to spew more shit, so I look at Damian and Alex and say, "Paperwork, now, and make sure you hand Basil the extra piece of proof that his man was involved."

Alex nods, knowing the cold killer is completely present; he knows my father's words have hurt me, and I've shut off my emotions. My mask is firmly in place. I look at my father again and say, "As far as I'm concerned, you died when my mother did. If I do decide to marry anyone, it will not count as an alliance between the Greeks and whoever I decide is the right fit for me."

All the men sit up straight, shocked by my announcement, some about to protest. They know no one will want Selene; her behavior alone is a turn-off, which means there will be no alliance with the Greeks, but I've got one better for them.

I raise my hand to ensure they all stay silent, just like my uncle is. I've already spoken to him about this; he knows Sergi does not want the throne, so this is the next best step, if he can't convince him, because he knows I won't get involved with the two of them. I'm aware of what Alex had to do for Juan to give up my location, and I reamed him for it. That wasn't fair to Sergi, even if he says it's fine because it damn well isn't, he isn't ready to meet his biological father.

I love my uncle, fiercely, but what he did to Sergi was cowardly. I've told him to his face more than once that their meeting in two weeks shouldn't be happening; it should be happening when Sergi is ready for it.

"It will be an alliance between who I chose and the Spanish Mafia." My father's face goes red while the rest of the men gasp in shock. Many have tried to get in bed with the Spanish, so to speak, but my uncle has always declined; he wanted family to take over, and my future husband will, if Sergi refuses to take his place as heir.

Ignoring my father's scowl, I look him in the eyes, and I continue, "Good luck trying to find an alliance with someone when everyone knows what Selene gets up to; I know you are aware of what she and Alex did."

He shakes his head. "They were engaged and would be married now if she hadn't messed up."

I tsk, mocking him. "Messed up? Do you mean lying to you and Alex to get back at him for not giving her his black card? They were still sleeping together after you changed the engagement over to me. I know you're aware of this, so I don't know why you're so shocked that I said, 'Fuck it', and left.

Do you really think I want a man who thought it was a good idea to continue to fuck my sister, the sister who tried to sell me for her drug debt? You sent me away because your brother tried the exact same thing; you killed him for it, and yet she does it, and suddenly it's okay? We're not close because you were a spineless coward, who I no longer see as family." He pales, and I turn and head back to my seat. Alex's rage is vibrating from him; he knows all this coming up is a setback, because now the thought of him even holding my hand revolts me. How the fuck did I think this could work between us? It can't. It really can't. I feel my heart break with the realization.

We're over.

I swallow hard.

"Gentlemen, in the folders I placed in front of you is proof of Mihai not only trafficking young children for some Cartel members, but also doing it in your territories. He picks the children up in your neighborhoods, and hands them over to someone in another of your neighborhoods, so if he is caught, you all will get the blame instead. He has fabricated it so you would be convicted instead of him; it seems he was the mastermind. Juan has had men looking into this, and it's been proven Christian was just the front man; Mihai was their leader all along."

Every man's face turns red.

"I am here today to gain votes to personally kill the fucker, which I should have done a month ago. What do you all say?" Every man at the table shouts *aye*, including my father and his most trusted guard.

I nod, then look at Sergi.

"Ice cream date?" I ask and raise my brow.

He knows what I'm asking, and he chuckles. "Okay, but you have to change, Phoebe Pie." I smile and nod, my giddiness taking over, making him shake his head. I hear my uncle clear his throat, bringing me back to the table. This is the first time he's physically listened to his son's voice, and my heart hurts from them both.

I pick up my phone and take it off speaker and say, "*Tio*, I will contact you tonight to go through the plan. Send my love to my auntie."

He clears his throat again, struggling to grasp his emotions. "*Si*, I will, sweetheart. You have fun with your cousin." Then he hangs up, before I sigh and send a sad smile to Sergi.

I place my phone in my hidden pocket, then turn and leave the conference room without looking back at all the men's eyes on me. I go down to Sergi's office, grab my bag, which I placed there the way up, and quickly change into my light pink off-shoulder top, a pair of dark blue jeans, and my favorite ankle boots. Placing my other clothes in the bag, I pick it up and head to the elevators, but when I get there, my father is also waiting. I go to turn toward the stairs when he spots me.

"You look different in those clothes."

I sigh, knowing I can't get out of this. The elevator pings as I get near, and we both enter. I ignore him and press the parking lot button, staring straight ahead.

He clears his throat. "I know you and your sister have your differences."

I scoff and look at him, stopping him from continuing. "Differences? She fucking sold me, and you're talking like all she did was steal my favorite dress! For years you have put her first, and while you spoiled her and gave her everything she wanted, including your time, which by the way, was the *only* thing I wanted, I was being hung from a ceiling in a warehouse by chains wrapped around my wrists, and told to *'get out of them, then you can eat.'* The first two months I only ate four or fives times; I would hang for days while in my own urine and feces, only allowed sips of fucking water."

His face pales, but I don't stop.

"As soon as my mother passed, it was like I didn't exist. Gone was the father who would swing me up in his arms, and read to me at night. You sent me away to live with a woman I barely knew, with no acknowledgment of the danger I was in. I'd only met her a few days before the funeral and had only spoken on the phone whenever she'd call Mom.

You knew this and yet sent me away anyway. You could have easily protected me but decided to take the easy way out. You think I didn't hear Selene bitching and moaning to you about me living back in my childhood home after *you* changed the arranged marriage over to me? You don't think I didn't hear you agree with her *every time*? She's a fucking drug addict after my inheritance, and you placate her continuously because she's your precious fucking daughter, while I'm the look-alike of your *dead wife*!"

I shout the last bit as his face goes red, about to open his mouth, but I'm not done. "Tell me, Father, have you ever hit her like you did me?" I don't think I've ever seen someone go from bright red to deathly pale so fast. "Remember when I threatened to run away if you tried to kill the cat my grandmother gave me as a congratulations for passing her tests with flying colors, and you smacked me for it? Did you know how close I was to getting my knife out of my boot and stabbing you in the neck with it?" His eyes look at me full of sorrow, but I don't let it affect me. He made his bed. "Did you know that you smacked a severely dangerous, trained killer and came so close to death, and the fact that you were my father was the only thing that kept you breathing?" I glare at him as the elevator dings for the parking garage.

I walk out, then stop and turn halfway and state, "Just so you know, you can't be a whore when you've never had a man touch you. I have only ever kissed two men in my life, Alexandr and a man from college, who I nearly killed after he betrayed me." I give him a raised brow while he looks at me in shock as I state my final say. "I'm still motherfucking pure, Father, perfect for an arranged marriage for the Spanish Mafia, don't you think?"

He steps out of the elevator as I get to my bike, his face now going red again, but I ignore him as I strap my bag down and sit on the seat. I turn her on and rev her, smiling a little, while my father watches me. I give him the middle finger and drive off.

Immature? Yes, Refreshing? Absolutely.

Ten minutes later, I arrive at the Brew Box, and I smile. Sergi told me all about this woman he met; she served him coffee on the day he found out I left. He was struggling, and she enticed him immediately without even meaning to.

I walk in and spot Sergi already sitting at a table with a beautiful woman, and I smile at how much love he has in his eyes for her. My heart hurts at the thought of this all going wrong for him. When he came clean about meeting someone who wasn't aware of our lifestyle, I pleaded with him to tell her, but so far, he hasn't, unfortunately.

I head over there, and both of them stand. I stick my hand out to the bombshell, who has no idea how pretty she is. She's in dark jeans and a brown long-sleeve t-shirt, with the coffee shop logo on the front left. Her extremely dark black hair, which seems to have a hint of blue, is up in a messy knot on the top of her head. Sergi says it's the first thing that he noticed; apparently, it's quite long, too. Her violet eyes, which have a hint of blue, look at me with kindness, making me smile wide.

"Hi, Avery, I'm Phoebe. It's so nice to finally meet the woman who can hold this knucklehead down." She giggles a little and smiles widely.

She takes my hand before I pull her into a hug, making her flinch and tense for a moment before she relaxes and whispers, "Thank you, it's nice to meet you, too." And I smile. She's had a hard life. Sergi mentioned she has no family and has struggled, but he has not given me all the details because he, too, is in the dark.

Apparently, she's slowly opening up to him, and I'm hoping we can become good friends so she trusts me enough to tell me, too. She's a beautiful person on the inside and out; she has that aura.

I look at Sergi over her shoulder as I squeeze her tight; she's smaller than me, with curves many females would die for.

He smiles, looking far happier than I've ever seen him, and I smile back. Man, Alex and Damian are going to be pissed that I met her first.

eighteen

Alexandr

I WATCH the love of my life walk out of the conference room, and I lose my shit; I swipe everything off the table in front of me in a rage.

My father looks ready to grab hold of me in a hug but won't because it's a sign of weakness with the Family heads in the room. I look at Basil and point my finger at him like there isn't a dead body on the floor next to him. Damn him for bringing this shit up right now when I'm trying to win my girl back.

"You need to get your fucking priorities straight, old man. The shit you just spewed was out of line; you're listening to a cokehead instead of getting everyone's side of the story, and you wonder why she doesn't want anything to fucking do with you?" His face goes red as Sergi stands to leave.

He looks at me and Damian and says, "As you heard, I have an ice cream date with my favorite cousin." I raise my brow; that was a nice little dig toward Basil because of Selene. He looks at his uncle, shit, his uncle, by marriage, but still, I chuckle a little, and he glares at me, reading my mind, then sneers at

Basil, "If I stay any longer, I won't be held accountable for my actions."

Then he storms out. Basil sighs, running a hand through his hair, and says, "Selene wouldn't lie; she has no reason to, either."

I let out a dark chuckle and state, "No reason except the source of her income; I take it she told you about when she came looking for me at the club two months ago, then? When I fucked her ass in the alleyway, trying to punish Phoebe for leaving me, not realizing at the time she was the cause for my girl leaving in the first place?" He pales. "You knew we were fucking. I told you it's the reason Phoebe left, but clearly, Selene told you it was false, so it *must* have been, right? Do I need to show you proof?

You were supposed to be watching her like a hawk to gain proof of her working with Christian, but now I think you were living in coocoo land and decided to bury your head in the sand."

Basil jumps up from his seat and says, "How fucking dare you talk to me like this? I am the fucking *Nonos*!"

I shout back, my patience gone, "Then fucking act like it!"

He growls in frustration and leaves. I sit and bang my head on the table, while the other men stay silent.

My brother is the first to speak. "It'll be alright, Al."

I chuckle darkly and lift my head. "She wouldn't even fucking look at me as she walked out, so how in the hell am I going to get her to forgive me before eleven months are up? I've only just got her to hold my fucking hand, doubt even that'll happen ever again now." I sigh, get up, and wave my hand, leaving the room and heading for my office, feeling fucking pissed and defeated. I won't see her tonight because she's decided to stay at her uncle's while in New York this week instead of my penthouse. If I stay at her ranch, it's with Ares in the spare bedroom.

I shut the door behind me and sit at my desk, sighing. I have plenty of legitimate paperwork to do, so that's what I will do. Hopefully, it'll clear my head.

A few hours later, I've made a dent in the paperwork, when my work phone rings. I know my secretary is not here today. I knew Phoebe was coming in, and I doubt she would have taken it very well seeing her here, too. I'm pretty sure if she knows about me making Candy my mistress, then she knows about the evening fuckfests I have with Bethany, Selene, and Mindy a couple of times a month. I really need to fire Bethany.

"Alexandr speaking."

"Hey baby, I've finally caught you. Where have you been? I have been trying to reach you, but one of the men made me leave my hotel room." Candy's whiny voice comes through the line, and I sigh. For fuck's sake, I can't catch a break. I run my hand through my hair before I realize I need to take out my frustrations, and I smile. A plan is forming. A plan that I didn't know at the time would cause me the most unbearable pain.

"Sorry, babe, I've been busy. And as for the hotel room, I decided to make something more permanent for you; it was supposed to be a surprise, but I found a nice three-story brownstone for us. What do you think?" She squeals on the other end of the phone, making me move the handset away from my ear. Why the fuck did I make her my mistress again? Oh yeah, to punish my girl for something I forced her to do.

"Oh, baby, that sounds amazing. Can we go see it today?" I chuckle. She sounds so eager; she probably thinks I'm the stupidest guy going. Well, to be fair, I used to be until Phoebe opened my fucking eyes.

"I can't today, babe; I have to go out of town again tonight, so it'll have to be next week."

She sighs. "I miss you when you're gone, and we haven't seen each other in a month. Can I still use your office while you are out of town? The guards wouldn't let me the last few times, and you know how

I like taking a nap in between my sets." She whines, and I smile, hook, line, and sinker. "Of course, gorgeous. I'll see you in a week, okay?"

She sighs happily. "Okay, baby, I love you so much."

I try not to gag, and hang up, then text the men at the club, granting her access to my office. I should expect a call in around, say, three minutes from my brother, asking what the fuck, and I smile; he'll love to be involved in this.

Two minutes and thirty-eight seconds later, instead of my phone ringing, my brother barges into my office, his face red from rage. I smirk and lean back in my chair, crossing my arms over my chest.

"That's impressive, brother; I expected a phone call." He growls at me, narrowing his eyes.

"What the fuck are you doing, Al? You have one setback and go to your mistress again, granting her access to your office, where she was stealing from us. Do you want to lose your woman and your fucking job?" I chuckle, making his face even more red.

"I have already ensured all paperwork and passwords are locked in the safe under the floorboards, a safe that only you, Sergi, Dad, and I know about. I thought we could finally get rid of a problem. You *are* my little brother." His eyes light up, his frown turns into a devious smirk, and I smile.

"Want to get some frustrations out tonight, do we, big brother?"

I chuckle, damn right, I fucking do.

"She should be fucking her drug dealer at roughly 9 PM, after they try to get into my draws and wall safe, so we have…." I look at the clock on the wall; it's nearly 5PM "…four hours."

He smiles. "Enough time to finish some meetings. I'll message Sofia so she knows I'll be late and that I'll be at the club. I don't want her hormones going haywire on me again, though if it were the other way around, there would have been blood spilled, so I do understand."

I chuckle. He slept on the couch for a week after visiting the club. He was there to check on things, but someone had sent her a picture of him talking to one of the strippers, which happened to be Savannah, who he let get off on him several times when Sofia was gone raising their little girl alone, so it was a sore subject. It turns out it was Misty, a new stripper who wanted the big boss and tried to ruin their marriage, so she no longer works for us, but is still alive, just in another country.

"I'll message Sergi, and we'll meet at the garage at 8:40 PM." He smiles, then walks out while putting his phone to his ear. "Hey *Malyshka*, how are you feeling?" I smile, proud of my little brother for getting his act together. Now, if only I could. I sigh. I really should have listened to him instead of thinking I knew better. I grab my phone to message Sergi.

> Me: 8:40 p.m. parking garage at Volkov & Co. we've got some unfinished business at the club. you in?

He messages back five minutes later. I've just finished some more paperwork and looked at my phone. I chuckle at his reply.

> Sergi: Fuck yes, about time, dickhead.

Another text comes straight through.

> Sergi: Phoebe says to count her in, too.

I laugh, which quickly dies when a thought comes to mind.

> Me: I don't think that's a good idea.

My phone rings, and I sigh. It's a video call. I answer it, and my beautiful girl's face pops up. She's in her normal clothes, looking beautiful, but her green eyes are burning lasers at me. I chuckle a little, making her eyes narrow at me.

"Do not make me hurt you, Alex. I want my fun!"

I chuckle again, then clear my throat, getting serious. "*Malen'kaya ptitsa*, she'll say things to rile you up." She sighs and looks ahead at something that makes my brows furrow as a small smile appears on her lips. Where the fuck is she, and who the hell got that little smile from her? My jealousy is going up a notch. My office door opens, and Damian walks in with some more paperwork. He frowns at me, noticing my expression, and walks around my desk to see what's happening. Phoebe looks back at the screen and gives Damian a smile.

"I know she'll say shit, but this is something I have to do, Alex."

I sigh, not able to say no, and look at Damian. "She wants to come tonight." He looks at her and nods. "Okay." She smiles big, then mischief shows all over her face, making both mine and my brother's eyes narrow. "I have a little payback for you two. I mean, I know Alex is technically the one who caused all the hurt, but you, Damian, knew what he was doing. I understand the whole 'he's my brother' concept, but you call me sister, and you should have kicked his ass for what he was doing, so you deserve a little punishment, too, just like Sergi, considering he is my blood cousin, and he still kept me in the dark about Alex's infidelities. Me showing you this will be his punishment, knowing you two will make his life hell, now have a look at who I met today."

She says with a grin, then turns her camera around, and Sergi comes on the screen with his arm wrapped around a beautiful woman with hair so black it almost looks like it has blue in it. Both Damian and

I look in shock, and then we get pissed. She's right; we're going to torture him.

"He introduced you first, the Angel of fucking Death," Damian rages while I say, "That's not fucking fair," while she literally cackles.

"See you in a bit, gentleman," she says, then hangs up.

I look at Damian and say, "I'm going to fucking kill him!" I sneer, and he growls, "Not before I fucking do!" Then storms out. Yeah, she dished out the right payback! And I bet there's more to fucking come. It's a good thing I love her!

At 8:35 PM, I meet Damian at the elevators; we're both still pissed that Phoebe met Sergi's girl first. I know she doesn't know about our lives, but we can dress fucking casually and hide our fucking weapons!

Once we reach the parking lot, Phoebe is leaning against my Mercedes, her leather gear on, while the traitor stands near my brother's SUV. We both walk over to him while Phoebe laughs her ass off, and Sergi just smirks as both Damian and I talk at the same time.

"Seriously, the Angel of Death can meet her, but not us?

"I was the fucking first person you told, for fuck's sake."

"I'm your best fucking friend."

"We've known each other for years; we're fucking family!"

He loses it and laughs his ass off, before getting in Damian's car, making us both scowl. I growled, walking over to my car and opening the door for Phoebe.

"Get in, you hyena."

She laughs harder, and I grab her hand, helping her up after she falls on the ground laughing, unable to keep my smile at bay. What a fucking infuriating woman! I help her into the car, go to the driver's seat, and place my hand in between her thighs while she still laughs. I shake my head and say, "You're lucky. I love you, my hyena."

She laughs harder again, making me chuckle.

Damian has already turned his SUV around, waiting for me to follow, so I ignore my hyena and start the car while stroking my thumb along her leg.

Twenty minutes later, we're pulling into the underground parking lot for our strip club, and we park near the elevators. All the men know not to acknowledge our presence, to not tip Candy off. We get out of our cars, and I put my arm around Phoebe's waist, grateful she doesn't move out of the way, and we head to the elevator and go up two floors. Once on the floor, Andrew, our doorman, lets us in with a nod, keeping his eyes off of my girl. He values his life. We head to my office.

I can already hear Candy's moaning mixed in with the music from downstairs, and I furrow my brow when I realize she sounds the same as when she was with me. She fucking faked with me? I scowl, and Phoebe snorts, noticing my look and making me narrow my eyes at her, but she just smirks at me, and I shake my head, moving forward.

I open my office door, and the sight that greets us is quite sickening, to be fair. Candy is on all fours, a fat, greasy man is fucking her ass, while Savannah is standing in front of Candy, holding her head to her pussy, and all my paperwork is messed up over my desk, where they've gone through it all.

Phoebe enters the room first and chuckles before she looks at me. "Seriously, that is what you tried to replace me with?" I smirk at her and playfully narrow my eyes, causing her to grin wide while my brother and friend snort, enjoying her roasting me, assholes. The three on the floor quickly get up in surprise when they hear us, as Candy starts to fake cry.

"Alexandr, baby, it's not what it looks like, I swear." Mascara rolls down her cheeks, and Savannah pales when she notices Damian, who's smirking while the greasy man freezes, his small dick getting smaller as it deflates, his face going ashen.

Phoebe chuckles when she notices him standing there frozen, butt naked, while Candy quickly covers herself with the guy's dirty shirt. Savannah goes to Damian like he can save her. Before she can get near him, Phoebe grabs her hair in a tight twist and pulls it down hard in her fist, causing Savannah's head to tilt back in an awkward angle. Phoebe then chuckles evilly. Candy is watching her, wide-eyed, not knowing who my girl is.

"Now, what kind of friend would I be, letting your skank naked ass anywhere near Sofia's man? You going over to Damian, *my brother*, for a reason?" she sneers.

Damian smiles at her words, loving the brother title. Savannah tries to yank her hair out of Phoebe's grip but cries out in pain. Instead, my girl smirks, and I must readjust my pants, causing Sergi and Damian to chuckle. Candy notices and smirks, thinking it's because of her, and walks toward me, before she wraps her arms around my waist and presses her sweaty body against mine before I can move. Now, I don't like hitting women, but come on, she's covered in the guy's fucking sweat. I hold my breath so I don't gag and go to move, but she tightens her grip and pouts at me.

I look up when Phoebe says, "Well, it looks like you're off the hook for a little while, Sav; why don't you sit next to Greasy there?" Savannah is shoved onto the couch. She lands face-first in the guy's cock, making Daman and Sergi lose it. I look at Damian and see he's recording everything for Sofia, and I have to bite my lip from smirking. I don't want Candy to get the wrong idea; it's bad enough that she has a grip on me.

She starts to whisper to me without realizing the danger she's now in.

I look down at her and glare hard.

"Let's go have a look at that house, baby. This here…I owed money, so I was just paying him back. That's all. I didn't want to worry you. Please, baby."

Just as she finishes, Phoebe leans over her shoulder and says, "Oh, so you haven't been stealing millions from Volkov & Co.'s businesses while Alexandr sleeps, after you've fucked or while you've been in his office alone? Millions which, by the way, have been transferred back from your off-chore account," she says so sweetly, you'd think she was shy and quiet Phoebe again and not the Angel of Death. I try to move from her grip again, but Candy holds me tight and pales. My heart rate picks up when I realize Phoebe won't look at me, and I know Candy's grip on me isn't helping the situation. I grip Candy's arm and move it from my waist, but her other hand grips my shirt, and I growl, but Candy doesn't seem to see the problem as she continues to bait my woman.

I look toward my brother, my eyes pleading for some help, and he starts to come toward us as Candy smirks, and he stops, seeing the killer in my girl's eyes, shit.

"Let me guess, you're the idiot who ran like a little baby? Well, I should thank you for leaving because you gave him to me. Do you know how fucking hot he is to fuck? He gets me wet so easily, and his tongue is dynamite."

I go still, completely forgetting about Candy's arm wrapped around my back, but Phoebe just smiles nicely at her.

"Well, it's a good thing I've never fucked him then, isn't it? I don't fancy catching any STDs."

I slowly close my eyes. A lump forms in my throat at her next words.

"I should thank you, actually, because seeing this helps me with the decision I was struggling with this morning." I go to grab her arm, knowing she's leaving me, but she moves away from my touch and doesn't look at me, and panic rises. I knew she shouldn't have come tonight. I look at my brother and see the panic on his face, too, and he starts in our direction again. I look toward Sergi next; he's standing behind Greasy to ensure he stays seated on the couch I'll be burning later. Greasy is next to Savannah, who's visibly shaking, and he looks uneasy, too.

I look back at Phoebe, and she's now looking at me. Peace washes over her face.

No, no! "*Malen'kaya ptitsa…*" I say, panic I can't hide straining my voice as I try to move out of this bitch's grip, a bitch who's smirking at the situation, probably thinking she's saved. Phoebe smiles at me, grabs her gun, and turns, shooting Savannah in the kneecap. Savannah screams out in pain while Greasy vomits on the floor. Great, now I've got to strip the wooden flooring, too.

Damian looks at Phoebe in shock, and she shrugs. "For Sofia," she remarks, making him grin wide at her. Then she puts her gun back behind her and goes to walk out. At the last second, she turns and looks at me. Candy's arm is still tightly gripping my shirt, her head near my chest as I'm leaning back away from her to stop the contact, and instead of shoving her to the floor, I just stand there with my arms hanging down like a fucking idiot.

"Goodbye, *Agapi Mou*," she rasps, then turns and leaves.

My heart feels like it's being torn in two. Both my brother and Sergi tense, knowing I'm about to blow.

I shove Candy off me, and she stumbles back. "Baby, wha—"

I don't let her finish as I grab my knife from the sheath behind my jeans and slice across her throat. Blood pours out of her neck, and she drops to her knees, looking at me in shock, her hands gripping her neck as she chokes on her own blood. Savannah screams, and I grab my gun, shooting her between the eyes. I look at Greasy, who's pissed himself and smells like he's shit himself, too, and is covered in his own vomit.

I approach him and he blabbers, "Look, man, I'm sorry, it was just easy money. Mihai offered me a higher rank to grab all your information. Candy was his mistress; please, dude, I'm—"

I stab him in the ribcage, shutting him up, then slice the knife up toward his neck, hitting his windpipe. I slice through it, and watch as he slowly dies in front of me. My whole body is now cold and numb from the mistakes I've made that not only risked our Bratva and Mafia but also my girl's love for me.

nineteen

Phoebe

I WALK OUT of the club with my heart in my throat and my face void of emotions, while on the inside, I'm dying. But this is the right decision. Seeing her arms wrapped around him and him not pushing her away, only gently trying to pry her hands off him, cemented it for me. I was already having doubts after having to remember him with Selene this morning—no thanks to my so-called father, but just now, it was a slap to the face. Even after he found out why I left, he still fucking slept around without a care in the world.

He must feel something for her to not push her away, especially with me standing right there. I wipe the lone tear that's fallen from the corner of my eye and start walking toward the subway. I need to get to my uncle's, grab my bag, and go home. I have a class in two days that I need to prepare for, and I have my heart to try and glue back together, even if I will forever be bound by him.

As I round the corner, my neck starts to tingle, and I mentally kick myself for not having my guard up and for having too much in my head because of

Alex. Before I can turn, someone comes up behind me. They wrap their arm around my neck, intending to crush my windpipe, while their hand thrusts a large knife into my left side. I feel like all the air has rushed from my body. I try to push the pain away, my training kicking in, and my motivation to end this fucker comes when he speaks, "Not so cocky now, are you, you little bitch. I wonder if I can fuck that loose cunt before you die."

Mihai.

I smirk and let out a pained chuckle, making his arm tighten around my neck, choking me while he rips the knife from my side, and thrust it again, two inches lower, before pulling it out again. Fuck, that hurts. I cough, and blood spurts out of my mouth, making me flinch, knowing he's caught my lung. Dying doesn't scare me; staying in a world where the love of my life has moved on and making a family with someone else *does*.

I bring my right hand up and grab the throwing star in my top; he doesn't expect it. While trying to breathe through the pain, with all my might, I scream and twist, and stab the star into his neck. He lets go of mine, the knife dropping to the ground, and quickly grabs hold of the star. I fall to the ground, my legs giving out, not able to inhale a full breath. I quickly grab hold of my gun from my back, and he takes his out, and both of us fire at the same time. My bullet hits him in the neck, and he drops to his knees, choking on his own blood, dead within seconds. His bullet hits my chest. I cough again, causing blood to trickle out of my mouth as I fall onto my back. I slam my head on the concrete.

"*Phoebe*," I hear someone shout, and then the next thing I know, Alex is leaning over my head. "Fuck, sweetheart, you're okay, you're going to be okay." I smile at him, then cough, and more blood comes out. My whole body has gone numb; that's good; there's not long left now.

"I-I-I lo-ove y-you."

Tears shine in his eyes, and he places his hand on my cheek, saying, "Baby, please don't give up; I need you, my *malen'kaya ptitsa*," and he kisses forehead. Sergi moves into view; he's putting pressure on the knife wounds, tears falling down his cheeks.

"Keep fighting, Phoebe Pie," he rasps. I lift my right hand and hold it against his cheek.

"I-I lo-love you, b-big bro-brother."

He sobs as Damian leans over me, a phone to his ear, barking orders while keeping pressure on my bullet wound. The bullet is lodged somewhere; I swear I can feel it, so it definitely didn't go through.

"Get my fucking wife here now, and hurry with the fucking car," he orders clearly and calmly, but his eyes tell a different story. He hangs up, putting his phone in his pocket, then puts his hand on my cheek. "Come on, sweetheart, don't give up now; don't leave us. Don't leave him."

A tear trickles down his face.

"I-I'm s-s-sorry, d-don't cr-cry."

He lets out a sob before Alex leans down and kisses my forehead again, whispering, "You can't leave me, baby. I owe you a lifetime of groveling. Please, Phoebs, don't give up on me." Tears now pour from his eyes, and I try to reach up, but my arms don't want to work. He grabs my hand, realizing what I want, and places it on his cheek.

"I-I'm s-s-sor-ry for no-not trying h-harder." He sobs at my words, shaking his head. "Ssso c-c-old."

He screams out, "Where they fuck are they!"

I look at Sergi, who is covered in my blood, his body shaking with sobs, and my eyes close, my body feeling weak.

Alex rubs my cheek. "No, *malen'kaya ptitsa*, stay awake," he rasps.

"Sooo ti-tired," I whisper, before a car comes to a screeching halt next to us.

I hear a female scream out but can't focus.

Dimitri comes into view, and his eyes go glossy, while Sofia shoves Alex out of the way and leans over me. She puts her fingers on my neck, tears streaming down her cheeks.

"Her pulse is weak; we need to go now!"

Just as Alex and Dimitri start to lift me, everything in me feels weak and cold.

Darkness descends over me before I whisper, "Alex."

I hear him roar out in pain. Then nothing—no pain, no hurt, no heartache.

Nothing.

twenty

Alexandr

I BREATHE HEAVILY, my rage billowing out of me.

Growing up, because of my ADHD, I've never managed my anger very well. My parents built me a gym in the basement for this exact reason because, as an adult, it's ten times worse. My whole body is vibrating; she said goodbye, fucking *goodbye*. I shake my head. Does she really think I'd let her go after our first hurdle? She knew this would be hard.

I hear my brother answer his phone. He curses something about Sofia being near the club and then hangs up just as Sergi speaks.

"Al?" he questions me while my brother observes me, knowing I'm a ticking time bomb. I shake my head again, and turn to chase after Phoebe, before she gets the first flight back to California. Damian and Sergi shout my name, then curse when I speed up, and they follow me, knowing our men will clean up my mess. I walk out of the club and look around the dark parking lot, when I hear a scream, then two gunshots, and I run. I can hear Damian and Sergi running behind me, and when I round the corner, pain like no other spears me through my chest.

My fault. This is my fault.

My woman, my heart, is lying on the ground, bleeding out, with what looks to be Mihai dead next to her.

"Phoebe!" I shout as I run toward her. Blood—so much blood. I kneel and lean over her. "Fuck baby, you're okay, you're going to be okay." She gives me a small smile before coughing, and blood comes out of her mouth. My whole world collapses.

She's dying. No, fuck, no.

"I-I-I lo-ove y-you."

Tears brim over, and I place my hand on her cheek. "Sweetheart, please don't give up. I need you, my *malen'kaya ptitsa*." I lean down and kiss her forehead as Sergi comes skidding to her left side, and puts pressure on two very large wounds, tears falling down his cheeks.

"Keep fighting Phoebe Pie," he rasps. She barely lifts her right hand and holds it against his cheek.

"I-I lo-love you, b-big bro-brother."

He sobs as Damian leans over her, a phone to his ear, barking orders while keeping pressure on the bullet wound in her chest.

"Get my fucking wife here now, and hurry with the fucking car." He hangs up. Sofia was already in the area; she wasn't happy with Damian going to the club and decided to come kick his ass.

Damian puts his hand on her cheek. "Come on, sweetheart, don't give up now, don't leave us. Don't leave him." A tear trickles down his face as a sob leaves me. I can't lose her, not now. Please, no, please.

"I-I'm s-s-sorry, d-don't cr-cry."

He lets out a sob, and I lean down, placing a kiss on her forehead and whispering, "You can't leave me, baby. I owe you a lifetime of groveling. Please, baby, don't give up on me."

She tries to reach up, but her arms don't move, and I grab her hand, realizing what she wants, and place it on my cheek. She's so cold.

"I-I'm s-s-sor-ry for no-not trying h-harder."

I sob hard, shaking my head. She's saying, bye, she can't, she fucking can't!

"Sssso c-c-old."

I scream, "Where the fuck are they!" I look down at my girl, and I can hear Sergi sob. Her eyes close, and I rub her cheek.

"No, *malen'kaya ptitsa*, stay awake," I rasp.

"Sooo ti-tired," she whispers as a car comes to a screeching halt next to us.

I hear Sofia scream but can't focus on her, my eyes staying on my love. Sofia shoves me out of the way, and I fall on my ass. She puts her fingers on Phoebe's neck, tears streaming down her cheeks, while my father leans over Phoebe with tears in his eyes.

"Her pulse is weak; we need to go now!" Sofia states firmly, trying to get a hold of her emotions.

My father and I go to lift Phoebo, while Damian and Sergi try to keep the pressure on her wounds. Suddenly, her eyes close, and I hear her whisper, "Alex", before her chest stops moving.

No, fuck no. Roaring out in pain, I start CPR, screaming, "Phoebe! No, please don't leave me!"

Sergi stands, holding his hands to the back of his head with tears falling from his eyes as my brother has heartbreak all over his face. My father bends forward, leaning his hands on his knee and sobbing. I lean forward and blow two big mouthfuls of air into her mouth, then continue compressions on her chest.

"Please, baby, please." Tears run down my face as Sofia leans over Phoebe's head, checking her pulse. I don't stop the compressions; I can't lose her.

"There's a pulse; we've got to move *now*." She shouts the last bit, and Dad and I grab my girl again, and carry her to the massive Mercedes SUV. We all get in, with Sergi driving, while I place Phoebe's head on my lap. Damian sits in front, getting his phone out and calling ahead. Sofia lays Phoebe's legs on her lap, keeping track of her pulse, as my dad sits behind us, leaning over to watch her, too.

As we speed off to the hospital, one of our men in a different car stays behind to clean up.

A couple of minutes later, Sofia cries out again, "She's lost her pulse again," and I quickly move so I'm kneeling behind the driver's seat and start the compressions again, murmuring, "Come on, baby, don't give up now—fight."

Another five minutes later, we arrive at the emergency entrance at General.

I haven't stopped the compressions, and when the door swings open and a doctor on our payroll takes in the carnage, he snaps to it.

"Right, let's get her on a gurney, now."

They quickly move her out and place her on a gurney, where they start their compressions. They bring the defibrillator out and, "Shock in 3, 2, 1, *clear*," the doctor shouts, and they shock her, then look at the monitor they attached during the compressions.

Still a flatline.

I put my hands behind my head and beg, "Please, baby, please."

My brother has one arm wrapped around Sofia, who's inconsolable. Damien's hand is gripping my shoulder, my father is gripping the back of my shirt, while Sergi is kneeling, tears flowing from his eyes, and he rasps, "Come on, Phoebe Pie, breathe."

The doctor shouts, "Again!"

He counts down and shocks her again, and the machine starts to beep. I drop my head and let out a sob.

"We have a pulse—move to the OR now!" the doctor shouts again, and they move as we all follow until we reach the 'restricted access' point, and a nurse comes up to us.

"You can't go any further. Please go to the waiting room, and if you're family, we'll keep you informed."

I growl, ready to rip her head off, when Sergi stands forward.

"I'm her cousin," he points to me, "that's Alexandr Volkov, her fiancé." She pales at my name.

"O-okay, I-I'll let y-you know more w-when we have m-more information," she stutters, then runs the other way while we head to the waiting room.

Damian takes a seat with a crying Sofia in his arms, and Sergi leans against the wall, while I stand in the middle of the room, staring at the doors, with my father standing right next to me. He has his phone to his ear, speaking to my inconsolable mother.

Two hours later, we are still waiting to hear something. I keep pacing, and Sergi growls, "I can't stand around any longer; call me if you hear anything."

We all look at him as he storms out, and I look toward my brother, only to find him already watching me with concern.

I hear, "Sweetheart." I turn to see my mother rushing toward me. She wraps her arms around me, and I let my head fall to her shoulder. As I fall apart, silent sobs wrack my body. My father's arms go around me, too, holding us both tight.

I can hear Sofia sob behind me as I cling to my parents like I'm a small boy again. They both let go of me, and my father grabs my face with both hands and whispers, "She's strong; she's a fucking fighter, so you're not going to lose her. She won't allow it, you hear me."

Tears glaze my father's eyes, and I nod as my mother moves toward me again. She's in sweats, looking less put together than normal, and she wraps her arms around me while Damian and Sofia walk over, and they, too, wrap their arms around me. My father keeps hold of my face as more tears fall from my eyes.

When the doors open, we all look to see a terrified nurse who clearly doesn't want to be here. I walk out of everyone's arms and toward her, and she shyly looks at me and says, "Phoebe Adino's family."

I clear my throat. "I'm her fiancé."

She nods, and she sees Sofia. Sympathy shines in her eyes when she recognizes her, and my heart stops. "The doctor wanted me to come out and give you an update. One of the knife wounds punctured her lung, and they've managed to repair it, but she has also suffered from internal bleeding. They are currently trying to find the source of the bleeding. She has coded several times during the surgery, including on the way to the OR. The second knife wound punctured her bowels, and they're trying to fix that so she won't be stuck with a stoma bag." She clears her throat, and my tears fall faster.

She coded several times.

"Baby, please don't give up," I whisper to myself.

"The bullet just missed her heart, and they are currently trying to find it as well. They believe that's where the internal bleeding is. She also has some damage to her esophagus; it looks like someone tried to strangle her, as well as severe bruising to the right side of her face, like she banged her head on concrete, so she'll most likely have a concussion. She'll be in surgery for several more hours, and that's only if her body can handle it; she's very weak at the moment and has lost a lot of blood. It's going to be touch and go, I'm sorry."

Then she runs out of the room, and as I fall to my knees, a roar of pain booms out while my mother wraps her arms around me. I know what the nurse was trying to say: Phoebe's brain has lacked oxygen; if she *does* make it, she may never wake up, and if she does, she might not be my Phoebe.

I sob, my body shaking. I feel my father's arms go around me, and I can hear Sofia's cries of pain. Being a nurse, she knows how severe the outcome with my girl could be, if she even makes it off the table.

twenty-one

Alexandr

IT'S BEEN another hour since the nurse came to talk to us. Damian called Sergi, and he's now just walked through the doors with a pretty little thing next to him, with dark black hair and violet eyes.

He walks over to me, where I am sitting on the floor, my back leaning up against the wall, and my arms hanging over my bent knees. His girl looks shocked to see the blood all over me and is quite scared. I know she's only just met my girl, but I understand why she's here; he's in love with her, and he needs her, so he brought her.

He kneels before me. while Damian sits with a sleeping Sofia in his lap. My parents cuddle up near the door, watching me with concern.

"Any more news, brother?" Sergi rasps, and I shake my head. He leans down, leaning his forehead against mine. "She's the strongest person I know; she'll make it out of this." I nod. "Have you called Basil and Juan?" I shake my head, and he clears his throat. "Call Basil, and I'll tackle Juan, okay?" I nod, grateful to him. I know how hard it must be for him to call the man who didn't want him.

I watch while he takes his girl to my parents, who are basically his parents, too, and introduces them. He kisses her forehead, whispering something, and she nods. Then he goes outside to make the call while she sits near my mother, who's looking at her with suspicion. I know I should address the look, but my mind is just not in the right frame of mind.

I get up and go into the corridor, get my phone out, and press call, but not to Basil. First, I need to call her lawyer. My mind finally clears again, and I'm back to thinking logically. I need to ensure Basil doesn't have power of attorney. I know she mentioned a few weeks ago about her ensuring he didn't, but I wanted to make sure, and then I need to call her friend in California before I tell Basil.

Twenty minutes later, after a call with her lawyer back in California, who was not happy about the wake-up call until he realized what the buzz was about, he confirmed who had power of attorney. I then had an emotional phone call with Abby, who couldn't stop crying, stating she's on the next flight here with Ares. I call Phoebe's father last, and he picks up after three rings.

"Basil," he answers, clearly wide awake.

I clear my throat. "I need you to come to General," I rasp.

"What the fuck, Alexandr? What's wrong?" His voice is full of concern.

"Phoebe was stabbed twice and shot in the chest by Mihai; they don't know if she'll make it," I choked out. I hear a loud noise; things being thrown as he roars out in pain. I close my eyes against the tears. He might not have done things right, but he still loves his daughter.

I hear Selene in the background asking sleepily, "Father, what's wrong?" but he ignores her.

"I'm on my way," he croaks, and I hang up and walk back toward the waiting room where I bump into Sergi.

"Juan is on his way; the call didn't go well." He sighs.

I nod, knowing the phone call would have been hard for many different reasons, and now I must add more pain to his already heavy-laden shoulders.

I deeply breathe and say, "You have power of attorney."

Sergi looks at me in shock as he shakes his head. I grab his shoulder before stating, "I've spoken to her lawyer back in California; she made sure to put it in writing four months ago, signed, and official. If she dies, brother, you get everything she has; she made it airtight, so her sister or father don't get a penny."

I swallow hard.

"The inheritance, Basil's house, everything will be yours; Juan signed off on it." He looks pale, like he's going to be sick, and I pull him toward me and hug him tight as I whisper, "It also means Basil can't pull the plug if she ends up on a ventilator; she's put it in writing that he is not to have any say in or knowledge about her care." I feel him nod against my shoulder, which has gone wet from his tears.

We hear the doors open, and his girl looks out, and when she sees us, her eyes brim with tears, his pain becoming hers. He pats me on the back and walks over to her, and she hugs him tight. I'm guessing she still doesn't know who we are yet. Fuck, I hope she doesn't leave him when she finds out, because he's probably the worst out of the three of us; he'll either burn the city to the ground or self-destruct.

I head back into the waiting room and lean against the wall. I tip my head back and sigh, closing my eyes. I stay like this for about twenty minutes, when there's a commotion. I look up just as Basil walks in, his eyes red, and fucking Selene right behind him, looking hopeful and smug. I scowl and walk toward them with Damian, my father, and Sergi at my heels. Thankfully, my mother, Sofia, and Avery—Sergi's woman—are seated at the far end of the waiting room.

"Any news?" he questions as I get closer. I shake my head, making him scowl. He snaps out, "This is bullshit; I'll go see what's happening."

He goes to walk away but I declare, "They won't tell you anything."

He frowns. "Of course, they will; I'm her next of kin, her father."

I sigh and rub a hand down my face. Things are about to get heated, and I haven't the strength to deal with this. "You're not her next of kin, and you do not hold power of attorney."

Selene pales a little.

I shake my head. Of course, she wants to see if she'll get her grandmother's inheritance.

Basil laughs darkly. "No offense, Alexandr, but you two never married."

Fuck, I hate the reminder that, right now, I should be married to the woman I love, but I fucked it up.

I look him in the eye and state darkly, "I never said it was me, Basil. You have no legal right to any information regarding your daughter. Four months ago, she legally cut all ties with you, and the paperwork is airtight. I already spoke to her lawyer, who explained it. There are specific instructions, including who can have knowledge of and any say over her care if she were ever admitted to the hospital. You and Selene are both on the restricted list."

"She fucking gave Juan power of attorney? That won't stick; we can say she was coerced into signing it." Sergi chuckles darkly, getting Basil's attention. "This isn't fucking funny, boy. My daughter may be dying. I need to ensure she gets the correct care and isn't kept on a ventilator for months. She won't want to be a fucking vegetable."

Selene chimes in, "We also need to ensure my grandmother's inheritance isn't given to the wrong people."

Sergi smirks at her. He looks like a deranged sociopath, still covered in his cousin's blood. His voice dark, he remarks, "Well, considering she made all these plans behind everyone's back, being coerced into signing shit won't stand, and as for her being ventilated, *if* she makes it off the operating table, *I* will decide what happens with her care. As for the inheritance, you, Selene, will be getting fuck all." Selene and Basil look at me, confused.

"My woman made her blood cousin her power of attorney. Sergi gets the final say, Sergi gets any inheritance, Sergi will own your house, and it seems as though he is also a blood relative to Athena, and the legal documents were personally signed by Juan as witness. That means, you two can't do anything."

Selene's face goes bright red, and I look at Basil and say, "I called you because she's your daughter, but by the shit you just spewed about her being a vegetable, and Selene instantly chimed in about the inheritance, you don't actually give a fuck. You let that bitch get in your head on the way here, as usual, listening to the evil one. That tells me all I need to know; stay out of my fucking way." I turn and take a seat. I lean forward and place my head in my hands. I feel someone sit next to me, and I know it's Basil.

He sits for about five minutes before he says, "I haven't listened to her; I just don't want to see my daughter on a ventilator, but I also don't want to lose her."

I nod but don't say anything, because I know the fucking feeling.

Two more hours later, the doors open again, and I jump up, knowing it can't be Juan yet. His flight is roughly eight hours.

I see the doctor, his scrubs covered in blood. My face pales, and I go to him with everyone else at my heels. He rubs a hand through his hair as he looks at me.

"It was touch and go; we lost her a few times on the table. I managed to save her large intestine and her lung. Her esophagus is badly bruised but should heal just fine, and she has a concussion, probably from a fall."

He rubs his face and his words filter through my head.... She died on the table...more than once. A tear starts to fall down my cheek, and I don't wipe it away.

The doctor continues, "The bullet was 1 mm from her heart; it was lodged in her chest cavity. She'd lost a lot of blood, but she survived the surgery." I can feel my knees going weak while I hear my mother and Sofia sob. I look at them to see my father holding them both. Avery is holding Sergi up, while my brother grips my arm. Basil stands there stone, still listening to the doctor list his daughter's injuries, and even Selene has gone pale, realizing the severity of the situation.

"The next 48 hours will be the most critical; she's not out of the woods yet." He clears his throat. "She is in an induced coma; we'll try weaning her out of it in 3–4 days, but I don't know if she will wake." My legs give out, but my brother is there holding me up as my father quickly grabs hold of my other arm as the doctor continues. "If she *does* wake up, we're not 100% sure she will be the same again; each time she had to be revived, she was losing oxygen to her brain. If she wakes, she may be *awake*, but she might not *be there*, or she may not have her memories or even her speech and motor skills. We won't know until she regains consciousness."

He reaches forward and squeezes my shoulder. "I'm sorry, Alexandr, but her chances are not great; all we can do is wait and pray that she fights."

Then he turns to leave as I roar out in pain, falling to the ground. My father and brother wrap me in their arms as I sob silently. I can hear my mother and Sofia wailing, and Basil shouting 'no' repeatedly, while Avery tries to help Sergi, who falls apart in her arms.

twenty-two

Phoebe

MY BODY HURTS, and my head is pounding. I try to open my eyes, but I can't. Why can't I open my eyes? I panic; my heart rate is accelerating. Suddenly, I hear, "She's crashing! Get the crash cart in here!"

"Phoebe?" Sergi? He sounds so far away; where is he?

"Phoebe, no!" Alex?

God, he sounds like he's in so much pain. I feel a jolt go through my body, and it suddenly goes quiet. Where did they go?

I don't know how long it's been, but I hear voices again, whispering in my ear while I feel a warm tingle on my hand and on my cheek.

"*Malen'kaya ptitsa*, come back to me, sweetheart, I need you; it's been too long since I've seen those beautiful green eyes. *S'agapó.*" I feel warm lips against the corner of mine. He said "I love you"; he learned Greek, my Alex, but he's struggling with something.

I try to wake up, but I can't; I was leaving him again, everything fading.

Suddenly, I hear Juan. "Come on, sweetheart, you need to open your eyes; Alexandr needs you. He's gone on a rampage, killing many Romanians with Sergi's help. We need you back, your family needs you." Why is Juan here and not in Spain? Fuck, why can I not wake up? My body is tired again, and everything fades.

Suddenly I heard shouting, "Where are you fucking taking her? Phoebe!" Alex is in so much pain.

"Alexandr, she's got internal bleeding; we need to operate again, or we'll lose her."

The voices fade. My body is relaxing again. My mind is fading.

Alex.

"Come on, my *mikrí prinkípissa*, you need to wake up now. Alexandr…he needs you, and Damian is struggling to keep him under control. And I need you, I need to make things right, my daughter. Please, I can't lose you, too." My father is sobbing, and my heart aches.

Daddy.

"Father?" I hear Selene and my father growls.

"I told you to wait outside."

She replies snidely, "She's still my sister."

I don't hear his reply; I'm fading again, stupid fucking body.

I hear someone crying softly. "You're my best friend. Please come back to us; we all need you. Sergi has lost it, and Alexandr needs you. Please."

Abby!

Fuck no, no fading—wake up! My body relaxes again, for fuck's sake!

"Phoebe Pie, I need you to wake up. I hate that I'm in control of your medical shit. I'm honored, but I hate it. I need you. You'll be living on this ventilator for the rest of your life if you don't fucking wake up. I'll never let them unplug you, so you need to wake up.

Al, he's falling apart, he barely sleeps, he's out of control without you. God, why did you have to leave the club that night?" He sniffs, and everything comes back to me. My heart starts to ache because my family is in pain. I thought leaving would be okay; I thought they'd be fine. That's why I wasn't afraid when Mihai attacked, but I guess I was wrong. I shouldn't have walked away; I should have kicked Alex's ass and fought for us, instead of walking away, thinking it would have been easier on my already fragile heart. "Avery, she won't talk to me; she found out about who we are and who I am…she looked at me in disgust and refused to let me anywhere near her. She didn't run, but she also hasn't let me in. I need you, Phoebs, so please wake up. Please."

I feel wetness on my cheek, and I know it's Sergi's tears. They need me.

Move body, move—*no*, don't you fucking dare, no fading. *No!*

I feel a presence leaning against my body—a body I know well, my Alex. I feel his head on my shoulder, and then I hear someone whispering, "Should we wake him?"

Sofia!

I hear another voice saying, "No, *Malyshka*, this is the only time he sleeps with his love."

Damian…he sounds so sorrowful.

Sofia sniffles. "She's been in a coma for too long, Damian."

He sighs. "I know, baby, but Al and Serg aren't ready to give up just yet, and neither am I. She's my sister; they may not be married yet, but she's still my sister."

Sofia sobs. "I don't want to lose my friend, and I really don't want Mila to lose her favorite aunt. She needs to wake up; if we lose her, we lose Al, too."

Hurt, pain, sorrow—my family is struggling.

Why can't I fucking wake up? I'm fading again.

Seriously?!

I feel a light touch across my face, and my heart hurts hearing Alex's soft cries.

"Sweetheart, *malen'kaya ptitsa*, please, *please*, I can't do this anymore. I need you. You're the reason I breathe, please. Come back to me, please. If you go, I go. Please, baby, there is no life without you."

I feel his body shake with his soft cries. He really *does* love me, and he needs me.

Everything starts to go black again. I'm fading. I try to fight it, but I can't.

Please, I don't want to disappear again. Alex needs me, please.

I hear shouting and banging. "Alexandr, calm down." Damian?

Alex's growls and shouts, "Calm down? Fucking calm down? Basil is trying to get power of attorney so he can switch off her fucking life support! I won't calm down!"

There's another crash, then a heart-breaking roar.

Alex!

twenty-three

Alexandr

FOUR MONTHS—FOUR LONG MONTHS—IS how long I've watched my heart and soul leave me bit by bit.

I've gotten revenge. Phoebe may have killed Mihai that night, but I've killed his inner circle, with the help of Sergi.

He's not doing so well. One night after our killing, we went back to his apartment, and Avery was waiting for him. They'd been having problems for a few months, and he'd been pushing her away.

It's not just me; this has affected him, too; he's struggling.

He was covered in blood, and she looked like she was going to pass out when she saw him. He finally told her who we were, and she walked away without looking back—well, more like she ran away, with how he treated her. He's been on a killing spree since, and stupidly fucked Mindy, after I told her we were done, when she tried to corner me at the club a week ago while I was there to grab the books.

She'd been hanging around, waiting for me. When I shut her and her scheme down, she decided to latch onto Sergi. I hadn't realized, because I was already walking out of the door. Only my love was on my mind. The problem was that Sergi was drunk, so he had no idea what he had done until the next morning. He's regretted it since, but somehow, Avery found out, and she messaged him, stating, 'I hope she was worth it.' She was willing to talk about him being an underboss to Pahkan and Don, but they're officially over now. Just like with Phoebe, other women are a big no-no.

For four months, I've had to watch my girl's heart give up more than once. She's had to be operated on because of internal bleeding, where she coded on the table again, and she's still on a ventilator. Basil has tried to gain the power of attorney, stating his daughter's mental instability. Apparently, he can't handle seeing her like this. I know she's lost a lot of weight, and she's deteriorating every day, but like, fuck am I letting him kill my woman!

I've just thrown the remote, smashing the TV, while Damian tries to keep me calm, but I can't focus. Every time she dies and has to be revived, a piece of me breaks with her.

"Brother, it didn't work; Phoebe knew what she was doing; he can't change it."

Frustrated, I walk over to her bed and sit beside it. I grab her hand and lean my forehead against it, and my troubles instantly fade, as always when I'm with her. Tears flow, and I rasp, "I can't lose her. I am not ready to admit defeat, brother."

He comes up behind me, placing his hand on my shoulder. "I know. Neither am I."

I don't know how long we stay like this, but I feel at peace with my girl.

I whisper, "Come back to me, sweetheart, please."

My brother squeezes my shoulder, when I suddenly feel a light stroke on my hand. My head pops up, and I look down, willing it to happen again, praying I wasn't imagining it.

My wish comes true, and a few minutes later, it happens again, this time, I see it move. I look up at her face. Her eyes are still closed, and her beautiful white-blond hair with fading pink highlights is spread across her pillow. I stand up and lean over her as Damian moves out of the way, thinking I'm having a moment. I gently stroke her cheek.

"Phoebe, baby, can you hear me? Open your eyes, *malen'kaya ptitsa*, and let me see you," I whisper, and I feel Damian move around the bed and come to her other side.

"Al?" he questions in confusion and caution, but I ignore him. I feel her thumb move again, and my heart races as her eyes twitch. Fuck yes.

I feel Damian tense. He sees her and grabs her other hand, giving it a squeeze.

"Phoebe?" he murmurs.

I rub my nose against hers. "I feel you, sweetheart. Come on now, you've slept long enough. Come back to me, come home to me, please. Open those beautiful green eyes for me."

Then it happens: her eyes slowly open, and she looks up at me, recognition and love shining through. My eyes start to water, and I realize she recognizes me. She removes her hand from my brother's grip, and goes for the tube that's down her throat.

I quickly grab her hand and say, "Y-you need to l-leave it in, baby, just f-f-or now." I'm stuttering, my emotions getting the better of me.

I hear Damian quickly press the nurse button as a sob catches in his throat. She lifts her hand to my cheek, stroking it, and I fall apart. I sob as I lean down and place my head on her neck. I cry for the fear and pain I've felt these past four months. She's finally awake.

She rubs her fingers through my hair, and I hold her tighter, my whole body shaking with relief as the door to her room opens, but I don't pay attention.

"Damian, what's going on?" Sergi questions.

Damian clears his throat, and rasps, "She's finally awake. I've called for a nurse."

I hear Sergi sob, then he shouts into the hallway, "Nurse! Nurse! She's fucking awake!"

I hear several footsteps as Sergi comes toward me, grabbing me, but I don't want to let go.

He whispers, "Let them take the tube out, brother."

I nod into her neck and pull back, looking into her beautiful eyes, glistening with tears. I wipe the tears away, kiss her forehead, and whisper in Greek, "*S'agapó.*" She taps her heart then points at me, making my tears fall faster.

She's awake.

I step back as the doctors come in to remove the tube. I look toward the door to see my parents, Basil, Selene, Juan, Sofia, and Abby, all standing there with panic radiating from them, but it's Juan who speaks, "What's happening?"

Damian answers, clearing his throat again, struggling with his emotions, and reaches out to his heavily pregnant wife.

"She's awake."

Sofia bursts into tears as Abby collapses to the floor. Juan heaves a massive sigh in relief, while both my wraps their arms around Sergi and I as we watch the medical team do their jobs. I don't bother looking at Phoebe's father and sister; I can hear Basil sob, probably with regret, since he was trying to switch off her life support. They remove the tube, and I hear her cough. My whole body trembles with the need to get back to her, but my father keeps a strong grip on me while my mother is in Sergi's arms, silently crying.

We all stand back while they start their assessment.

The doctor comes to me after he's finished. "She's doing good, a lot better than we could have ever hoped. She remembers everything, including the incident. She has a long recovery ahead of her, but she's breathing on her own, she's talking—a little slower than normal, but that's expected after being in a coma for so long. She's going to be ok.

I will come back in a little bit to check on her again, do some X-rays, and order another MRI and CT just to make sure everything is as it should be. If everything goes as I suspect, she could be out of here in a week or two." He squeezes my shoulder, and then walks out.

I look back at my girl and see she's already watching me, and there's pain and sorrow in her eyes.

My love.

She lifts her right arm, extending it to me, and I go to her willingly. I grab her hand, and she gently pulls me to her. I lean down, place my head into the crook of her neck, and silently sob, not believing she's really awake.

I hear Damian and Sergi telling everyone to give us space. Most protest, but they give in. I then hear shuffling, and the door shuts, and I know we've been left alone. I hold her tight while she wraps both arms around my head, holding me just as tight.

And finally, after four long months, I heard her voice again.

"I'm okay, *agapi mou*, I'm okay."

I just shake my head and whisper into her neck, "Four months—that's how long I've had to live without you. For four months, I was petrified you would leave me forever. If you'd left, I would have followed."

She holds me tighter, and I feel her tears on my neck. Then her grip loosens suddenly, and I shoot my head up, worried, ready to call the doctor back, and she smiles slightly.

"Just tired," she rasps, her throat still scratchy from the tube.

I nod and lean my forehead against hers, and I slowly close my eyes, then open them when she cups my cheek and whispers, "I'm still mad at you for everything...you did, and you still have a lot of groveling to do, but I love you so much that I never...want to hear the....pain you were in ever....again. My soul is bound...by you, and I heard a lot while...I was in a coma. Your pain was killing me.... I knew I had to fight to come back to you and take your pain away. I-I love you."

Tears fall from her eyes, and a sob catches in my throat. I love her words but hate how raspy she sounds, and how much she struggles to speak.

"I'll spend a lifetime making up for my mistakes; you'll be treated like the queen who holds my heart, because you are," I whisper while staring into her eyes.

I place a gentle kiss on her lips, and then climb onto her bed. I lay her head on my chest, holding her carefully but tight, and whisper, "Rest, *moya lyubov*," then place a gentle kiss on her head while she holds onto me tight. I wait until her breathing evens out, then fall asleep, peacefully, for the first time in so long, because I finally have my woman back in my arms.

twenty-four

Phoebe

I DON'T KNOW how long I sleep, but when I wake up, the sun is setting. At some point, we must have moved because now Alex is holding me tightly, his head in the crook of my neck. I can feel the warmth of his breath as I run my fingers through his hair.

Hearing his pain on and off while I was in a coma destroyed me. I meant what I said—he has a lot to make up for, but I cannot live without him; I need him, and losing me would end him, and that would destroy me.

I hear a noise to the right and look to see Damian and Sergi sitting there, watching me. Both have unshed tears in their eyes that are full of pain. Despite my leaving for five months, they still care deeply about me and my family.

I break the ice, wanting to make them smile. I rasp, "Well, isn't this a little creepy?"

They don't smile, instead, Sergi's tears fall, while Damian fights his, so I rasp again, "I'm okay."

Damian shakes his head and stands, walking over to me on the other side of my bed, while Sergi stays where he is, trying to get a grip on his emotions. Sergi looks like a wreck; his usual slicked back hair is messy on top, a little longer on the sides than normal, and he's now sporting a beard.

I look away from him as Damian comes into view. He leans down and places a kiss on my forehead, looks at me as tears start to slip from his eyes, and my heart breaks. Our leader shows me his vulnerability.

He whispers, "Losing you would have destroyed us all, but it and would have killed him; I wouldn't have just lost my sister, I would have lost my brother, too."

My tears fall, and I rasp, "I'm okay."

He nods, grips the back of my head, and holds it against his shoulder, hugging me. I grab him tightly.

The movement wakes up Alex, and his hold on me tightens. He looks up at me, his eyes watering again.

"I wasn't dreaming," he whispers as Damian pulls back and places a hand on his shoulder.

I place my hand over Alex's on my cheek, and I repeat, "I'm okay."

He just shakes his head and looks to his brother, who does a subtle head tilt toward Sergi. I look and notice how he's gripping the arms of the chair so tight that his knuckles have gone white. Alex gets up and goes to him, while I feel useless for being unable to move.

Alex leans over him, gripping his neck, and whispers something in his ear, making him nod as more tears fall from his eyes. Damian stands near me, arms crossed over his chest, worry and concern for his family showing through his eyes.

Alex moves out of Sergi's way, and he finally gets up, coming to me. My tears fall faster as he leans over me and holds me tight. I feel wetness on my neck as he sobs silently, and I hold him tighter. After a few minutes, he calms down, and I whisper so only he can hear me, "I'm okay, and I'm going to help you get your girl back."

He shakes his head, lifting it as tears run down his cheeks.

He rasps, "I was hurting, so I pushed her away before she found out the truth, and then she walked away when she did because I was a dick about it. I fucked up even more when I slept with Mindy."

I lean away from him and narrow my eyes. I hear Damian clear his throat while Alex snorts, obviously happy I haven't lost my killer glare. Sergi keeps eye contact and braces himself, knowing what's about to happen—something he probably prayed I'd be able to do.

You can hear the echo of my slap in the room. Sergi straightens and rubs his cheek, and I shout, not caring about the pain it causes me in my chest, side, and throat.

"Mindy?! Fucking *Mindy*! Are you *kidding* me, Sergi, you fucking *moron*!"

Damian bursts out in laughter while Alex's face turns red, trying to hold his in. I narrow my eyes at him, and he lifts his hands in surrender, then walks over to me while Sergi looks at me sheepishly.

"*Moya Lyubov*, he was struggling; your father was trying to get power of attorney for you, and his girl had just left him, and he was drunk."

I nod, making him think I understand, but then I grab the cup from the bedside table and lob it at his head.

He ducks just in time, again trying to hold in his laughter, his eyes shining with love, amusement, and hope, now that I'm awake and his worst nightmares are gone. This is probably the most he's smiled since I nearly died. I try not to show my amusement, and keep my mask in place.

This idiot needs a good kick in the balls, fucking Mindy.

"I don't give a fuck if I had *died*, that is no fucking excuse." I look back at Sergi, who is staring at me in shock.

"You fucking moron, all she needed was a little time; if I wasn't in this bed, I'd kick your ass, then go and blow Mindy's fucking head off," I growled. "She wants a high-ranking husband. Please fucking tell me you wore protection." Alex can't hold his laughter in any longer, while Damian is literally on the floor in tears, and I must admit, I'm so fucking glad they're laughing. Seeing and hearing their pain was heartbreaking, especially Alex's.

"I only fucked her ass with a condom on, and took the condom with me. It's all on CCTV." He clears his throat while I gag, not wanting that visual.

I state, "I swear to fucking God, Sergi, when I'm at my full health, I'm kicking your ass!"

Chuckling, Alex walks over to me and sits on my bed. He leans down and presses a kiss on my head. "Calm down, *malen'kaya ptitsa*. I can see the pain in your eyes. Please, you've only just woken up. I don't want you to have a setback, please."

My eyes soften, and I nod, leaning into him as he wraps his arm around my shoulder. I look at Sergi; he looks like a fucking mess.

"I will help as much as I can, but you being with another woman…." I shake my head and rasp, "If the way she looked at you was anything to go by, you destroyed her; she looked at you like you were her whole world. If you want her back, you need to fight." He nods, and I can see the pain and a lot of determination in his eyes.

Alex clears his throat. "Just don't go about it the way we did, because watching your whole life bleed out in front of you and then waste away in a coma for months, I don't recommend it." I can hear the pain in his voice, and I place my hand on his cheek, and he looks down at me.

"I'm okay," I murmur, and he nods as a tear slips down his cheek.

I wipe it away, my big badass *brigadier*.

We spent the next half an hour brainstorming, before my uncle storms in. Sergi doesn't even look his way, and my heart breaks for him. I was hoping they'd have talked by now, with me being in a coma.

"I've given you enough time with her; now it's my turn." He looks at Sergi for a second. Pain enters his eyes, then he looks at me and narrows them. "You ever fucking do this to us again, and I'll kill you myself." The men chuckle and, despite not wanting to, Sergi can't help but laugh with them.

I shake my head at Uncle Juan as he walks toward me. He leans down and places a kiss on my head.

"Don't fucking scare me like this again; your men, your family, they need you, especially Alexandr. I've never seen someone go off the deep end as badly as he did. And your aunt, she was distraught. We can't lose you."

I nod and hug him.

"I'm sorry, *Tio*."

He nods, then turns to Sergi, who isn't looking at him. He sighs before sitting in the chair near him, making me smile. He's not giving up. Alex strokes his fingers through my hair, and I look at him and smile. We have a long way to go, but it's safe to say that nearly dying puts things into perspective. I just wouldn't recommend it.

He still has a lot of groveling to do.

My smile quickly vanishes when the door opens again, and my father walks in with Selene, the Volkov clan, coming right behind them, with Abby trailing. My eyes soften at the sight of her, and then a heavily pregnant Sofia with Mila holding her hand enters the room.

When Mila sees I'm awake, she screams out, "Phe-Phe!" and she runs toward me.

Alex helps her up, and she wraps her arms around my neck, starting to cry, her little body shaking. My tears fall as I hold her close. I look up at Abby and Sofia as they come over, too, and Alex moves to stand next to his parents as they wrap themselves around me, crying.

When they pull back, Mila keeps hold of me, and I place my hand on the baby growing in Sofia's belly. The baby kicks me, and I smile while Maria, Alex's mother, comes forward with Maksim, and he starts to push away from her to get to me. I look at her in surprise as Dimitri walks up behind his wife, before she places the beautiful boy on me, and he hugs me tight, too. He's a chunky little nine-month-old, and a spitting image of his dad.

I hold him just as tight.

"Did you really think we wouldn't bring him to see you or show him pictures? You are his aunt, and we missed you," Maria whispers with tears in her eyes.

I reach over and grab hold of her hand, overwhelmed by everyone, and I rasp, repeating myself, "I'm okay."

They both nod, and Dimitri bends down, kissing my forehead.

He whispers, "I can't take seeing you like that again, Phoebe. No parent should see their daughter like that, and you *are* my daughter; you hear me." I sniffle and nod, giving him a small smile as he runs his hand down the back of my head. I've never felt so grateful to have these people as part of my family.

After a few minutes, they both take the children. Mila cries, not wanting to leave me, so Alex walks over to her, picking her up from his mother's arms. "I promise, sweet girl, you can see your *tetya* again in a few days; she just needs to rest, okay?" He kisses her forehead. She nods and goes back to her grandmother, and my heart feels ready to burst at the love they're all showing me, and the fact he's calling me her aunt in Russian—so much love.

His parents leave with the kids, and Sofia sits down on her husband's knee as Abby sits on the other chair, while Sergi stands near the back wall with Juan sitting next to him. I withhold a chuckle, and he narrows his eyes at me, but I give him the most innocent smile. He just shakes his head. Alex sits near me on the bed.

My father comes into view, tears shining in his eyes, eyes that hold pain, regret, and love. I'm glad he gave the Volkovs the space they needed to see me. It was probably hard for him, but he knows they're more of my family than he has been. Selene follows behind him; she has the biggest scowl on her face, clearly pissed she couldn't get the inheritance. Even though it would have gone to Sergi anyway, I fucking made sure of it when I left.

"How are you feeling, *Mikrí prinkípissa*?" A tear leaks down his cheek, and I lift my arm a little as he walks over, grabbing my hand. I pull him toward me and hug him tight.

"I promise I'm okay, Daddy." He sobs, and my heart breaks. He's made many mistakes and let himself be manipulated by my sister, but he meant the best for me.

Plus, he's still my father.

When he pulls away, I wipe his tears, and he whispers, "I'm sorry for everything."

I nod and wipe my tears as I rasp, "It's okay."

He just shakes his head, and then sits on the edge of the bed, keeping his hand in mine.

Selene walks forward and leans down like she's going to hug me but sneers instead, "The slut lives. Shame father couldn't take over your care; you'd be gone, and I'd get what was owed to me." She obviously hasn't considered that everyone can hear her.

Every person in the room tenses except me. I chuckle. "A bit hypocritical, aren't we, Selene? A slut…really? How many people have you fucked?"

My father's face is red, and just when I think he's about to bite my head off, he gets up and twists toward Selene, shocking the shit out of me when he points at her.

"How fucking dare you? She nearly died. I tried getting power of attorney because I couldn't stand the thought of seeing my daughter on life support, not for the fucking money. And if she had died, the money was still going to Sergi; he has more rights to it than your spoiled ass. You weren't seeing a penny of it, and you're not owed a thing!

I have been blinded by your disgusting behavior for too fucking long, and I have had enough. You should feel grateful your sister allowed us to stay in our family home, considering it's in her name."

Selene's mouth hangs openly in shock, and her eyes hold panic when she realizes she didn't whisper what she said.

My father shouts, "Marco, Colin, Peter!" The three guards enter the room. When they see me awake, they visibly relax and release a relieved breath, and I smile at them so they know I'm good. Marco was always kind to me growing up, Peter was like a father figure, and Colin, well, he's my trusty spy and pseudo uncle. Colin and Peter tears in their eyes, while Marco smiles widely, and I place my hand on my heart, tapping it twice to Colin, and he does the same, as Peter walks over and kisses my head.

I smile at him, and then look at Colin again. You can see the guilt in his eyes. Blaming himself for Mihai getting to me. I tilt my head and give him a little head shake. He smiles, knowing I'm telling him not to blame himself. Alex squeezes my shoulder, and

I look at him smiling, and he chuckles silently when he realizes Colin is my informant.

He looks at Colin and mouths, *'Thank you.'* Colin nods slightly, a bit of guilt still in his eyes, making me scowl at him, and he chuckles a little.

Damian sees the exchange and smirks, shaking his head. Neither of them will say anything, so our secret is safe. What he has been doing would label him a traitor, but I'll kill anyone who tries to harm him.

My father gains my attention again when he says, "Take Selene home and make sure you take her car keys and all the cards and cash in her purse; she's cut off. She can get a fucking job." Then he looks at Selene, who looks like she's about to protest, and pales when he says, "You have thirty days to find another place to live. The only reason I'm not gutting you is because you're my daughter, but you fucking disgust me. When you learn to grow a fucking conscience, you will be welcomed back to the family. Until then, fuck off out of my sight."

Marco and Colin carry Selene out of my hospital room while she protests, apologizing over and over, stating she just needs a little fix, and I can afford it. My father ignores her and leans down, kissing my head and saying, "Get some rest, sweetheart; I'll be back tomorrow. I have to change all the bank passwords." He leaves with Peter following him.

The door shuts, and I look around. Everyone is holding back their laughter.

I state, stunned, "Did that just happen?"

Alex chuckles. "Yeah, baby, it did."

I shake my head. "What fucking universe did I wake up in?"

Everyone laughs their asses off.

twenty-five

Alexandr

FOUR WEEKS—THAT'S how much longer she had to stay in the hospital, and I barely left her side. She contracted an infection and had to stay for three more weeks. It killed me, but it also gave me a chance to finish the redecoration of the farm I bought my girl in the Adirondack mountains, after she'd agreed to give me a year to win her back...before she nearly died. With the help of my men and my family, we basically had it stripped and remodeled. It looks amazing.

Sofia went into labor in our new living room; our new niece weighed only six pounds and is absolutely perfect. She's the second child I've had to help deliver. They named her Aurora Victoria Volkov, and Sofia's mother burst into tears when she heard the gorgeous girl was named after her. Sofia's mother has come a long way, and she and Sofia are closer than ever.

Phoebe's been home for about a month. I brought her back to my penthouse to recuperate before I shocked her with her new home. She's been getting her strength back every day, and I've ensured she hasn't been bored, and enrolled her in vet school at the University of the Adirondacks. She's been doing the coursework at home, but the practical starts when we move. She doesn't know we're moving yet; she thinks she has to commute. I thought it would take a lot to convince her to move back to New York, but it didn't.

When I brought it up a week before being discharged, she shocked the shit out of me because she smiled and stated, *"I've already signed the farmhouse over to Abby; she wasn't too happy but understood that we'll FaceTime every day and visit when we can. If we want this to work, then we need to try harder, which means me coming home."* Then she kissed my lips softly, all while my love shined brighter for her.

Phoebe brings me out of my mind when she asks, "Are you going to tell me where we are going? I thought you were taking me to the university, but you drove past it."

I chuckle and squeeze her thigh where my hand has been since we started driving. My cock twitches.

Fuck.

I have the biggest case of blue balls going. I haven't seen any action apart from my right hand since Phoebe came back into my life; that was roughly six months ago, but I want to do it right.

When we get to our destination, our whole family will be there, including Avery, which was fucking hard, convincing her to come. She hasn't seen Sergi in nearly three months, despite him trying. But for Phoebe, she said yes, because they've become close. I've also got a minister at the new house. Dad managed to get us a marriage license with help from someone on our payroll, bending the rules for us, and I'm marrying my woman today. She just doesn't know it yet.

We get to the gate cutting off the road to the farmhouse, and the guard lets us in. Phoebe looks at me in confusion as we pull in. It sits on over twelve acres of land, with a built-in security fence. I filled those acres with four horses, some pigs, goats, a couple of dogs. There's also Ares, who had been staying with me since Phoebe's attack, and I even bought Goosy off the old man in the farmhouse opposite Phoebe's in California.

She may kill me for this, but when she graduates, she wants to have her own practice at her own farm, so I ensured a building was built three miles away from the house, with an apartment above. Abby even said, once she graduates, she'll move into it and work for her friend. She said the farm isn't the same without Phoebe, and she'll likely sell it and give the money back to Phoebe. I just chuckled; like hell, would my woman accept a penny of it.

We pull up to the beautiful house as Phoebe whispers, "Wow."

I smirk, then look at the house. It's a white, three-story house with a wraparound porch, decorated with white ribbons and balloons for our wedding, which she has no idea about. I turn to her again, placing my hand on her cheek to turn her head my way, and when my eyes connect with hers, I whisper, "It has eight bedrooms, eight full baths, and one half-bath on the ground floor. The master bedroom is on the third floor; it's the only one on that actual floor, with his and hers walk-in closet in an adjoining room. The bathroom has a walk-in shower and a jetted bathtub that fits at least five people. The second floor has four bedrooms, all of which have smaller walk-in closets and baths with a walk-in shower, too. And on the ground floor, we have another two bedrooms—I turned one into a mother-in-law suite, and the other into an office, removing the shower and bath, but leaving a toilet. There's an open-plan living room and kitchen, with a dining room off to the right-hand side, and a breakfast bar in the middle, creating a wall between them. And the basement has a bedroom that I stripped and made into a movie/playroom for our nieces and nephews. Again, I removed the shower and bath, but kept the toilet.

There's a pool out back in a fenced yard. I put a nice play set up, with slides, sandboxes, and swings for when the kids come over. And you have a barn full of animals, and inside the house are two dogs that you need to name, as well as Ares—oh, and I also brought you Goosy. A few miles down the road is your brand-new veterinary practice, full of all the appropriate equipment, with an apartment above that Abby has dibs on."

Taking a deep breath, I peer into her eyes, pouring all of my love into my gaze.

"Welcome home, *Malen'kaya ptitsa.*"

She has tears running down her face as she launches herself at me, pressing her lips to mine. I kiss her back with as much passion as I can. I slow down after a few minutes because I can feel myself getting harder, and soon, I won't be able to stop myself, so I lean my forehead against hers.

I whisper, staring into her beautiful eyes, "Marry me."

Her tears fall faster, and I continue, "Make me the happiest man and become my wife. Let me hold you every night and wake up to you every morning, let me give you children we can raise on this farm together. Marry me."

She lets out a sob and nods frantically, before I pull the red ruby and diamond ring out of my pocket and place it on her finger. This time, I kiss her with more fire.

I'm finally getting my girl.

After a little while of holding my girl, I help her out of the Mercedes SUV and walk her around the grounds. I take her to the barn to the left of us, and show her all the animals. She squeals in delight, seeing them all, making me chuckle.

Angel of *what*?

Then she goes to pet—yes, fucking pet—Goosy, before we head back to the house. I skip showing her the garden, knowing it's all decorated for the wedding. The pool is covered, so we can walk on it, and there's an arch filled with flowers at the end of the yard, with chairs on either side to make an aisle. Sofia has put petals on the ground as a walkway, too. I want to surprise Phoebe, and I also don't want her to back out if her mind wanders to my mistakes, like I know it does sometimes. When we reach the front door and I open it, a loud cheer erupts from our living area, where our family stands. The women have tears in their eyes and, to be fair, so do some of the men. Knowing we could have lost her, in a way, this is our miracle.

Her father walks out among the men, and she goes to him willingly and hugs him tight. After she was released from the hospital, they sat and discussed everything. Selene was the main problem with their relationship. Selene was jealous of how close they were before their mother died, despite having all of her mother's attention. When Phoebe was sent away, Selene got all the attention and loved it; she took advantage of it as she got older. I look to the side, and see her standing away from others with a scowl and what looks like a little bit of sorrow in her eyes. I just don't know if it's because this could have been her life—well, part of it, because I never would have fallen for her, and would still be fucking around—or because her sister doesn't spare her a glance.

I shake my head.

I understand why Basil brought her with him, but I don't think he understands the repercussions of his actions if she causes any shit. My woman is back to full health now; she still needs regular check-ups, but she's already gone on a couple of missions to stop the cartel from getting their purchases from some of the Romanians that are left after Sergi and I went on a killing spree. Someone else has taken over and decided to stupidly continue human trafficking, mainly children under the age of sixteen.

Phoebe was pissed and got back to the gym before she should have; we argued a bit about it, but as usual, she won. I'm a sucker for her, and I ended up being her fucking sparring partner. I've never been so hard, sparing with my woman. Hopefully, she doesn't shoot her sister today; that would be messy but one hell of a wedding memory.

I pull my girl back into my arms, and her father chuckles. My mother comes up to us and looks at me. I know what they're all waiting for; they know what I was doing today. That's why we're all here, so I lift her left hand up and kiss the ring, and my mother squeals in delight, while everyone cheers and claps. Then the women, except for Selene, who is now glaring at my woman, whisk my wife-to-be to the basement, making me scowl and the men laugh. I shake my head, then head up the stairs to our new bedroom to change into my tux, with Damian and Sergi close behind. All our guests head outside to the yard, where my girl will hopefully meet me.

twenty-six

Phoebe

AFTER SHOWING me around this beautiful house and getting the surprise of all our family, Abby, Sofia, her mom Victoria, Avery, and Maria dragged me away toward the basement.

I look at them, confused, until we get to the basement, and I see the wedding dress I originally picked to marry Alex months ago. I spin around to look at them in shock as Maria smiles softly.

"Upstairs, there is a minister, and the yard has been decorated. What do you say, Phoebe?"

Tears stream down my face again.

He wants to marry me *now*.

I look back at the beautiful dress. It's white, which is fitting, I guess. Still can't believe I nearly died a virgin. For over a month, I've been doing everything I can to get him to sleep with me, but nothing, *nada*. I thought maybe he was still getting it elsewhere, which was difficult for me to process, then I remembered he put a tracking app on his phone, and more times than I can count, I checked it. I always felt guilty, and he normally came home to me crying about it, because I still couldn't fully trust him. He would hold me and tell me it's okay, and it keeps my mind at peace. Things will take time; we still haven't really spoken about our past, not wanting to rock the boat, so to speak, but I know we need to, especially before we get married. But now I don't think we have time because he's thought of everything I might need for today so I don't back out.

I guess he wanted to keep our original plan and wait for our wedding night to have sex, and that's why he kept putting me off. I could kick myself for continuing to punish him his past actions. At least he'll get a nice surprise ,when he realizes that I am, in fact, still a virgin.

The dress is gorgeous; it has beaded lace with a sheath skirt, spaghetti straps, and a sweetheart neckline. The buttons on the back are pearl buttons, and it has a matching tulle overskirt. It's not flashy or in your face, it's simple, and I love it. I never cared about having a massive or over-the-top wedding, I just wanted my groom. I turn to look at Maria, and she has hope in her eyes, and I know, without a doubt, that even though it'll be painful to relive the past, I will still want to marry him…because I am bound by him. He's my everything, so I nod frantically, words escaping me, and she wipes her tears and takes me over to the dress.

They all help me get dressed. Sofia does my hair, curling it a little, then adding a flowered crown, then my matching veil to the crown. Avery, who has tears in her eyes, does my make-up light. She's happy for me but sad for what she's lost, because her love made stupid mistakes.

When she's finished, I take hold of her hands and give them a little squeeze. She smiles a watery smile at me, and I lean forward and kiss her cheek, whispering, "Have courage." She nods. She's confided in me a lot over the last month; she spent much time with me, and I know how much her heart hurts from Sergi's betrayal. She's said before that the Bratva stuff, despite being shocking, was something she could look past, after she really thought about it. In her mind, the men he killed were horrible human beings; they were and still are to this day kidnapping children, but it's the fact he slept with Mindy she can't get over. He betrayed her, and she's had one too many people betray her in her life.

She helps me stand, and I look in the mirror and smile brightly. I'm finally ready. I look toward Mila, who is sitting, watching a movie in her fluffy white dress, looking gorgeous. My heart is full. The women stare at me, their eyes shining, knowing this is a miracle.

I shouldn't have survived with only a few scars to show for my near death; I should be dead or brain-dead.

There's a knock at the door, and I see my father come in. When he sees me, he stops, placing his hand on his heart before he walks over to me and kisses my forehead.

"You look beautiful, sweet girl." I smile at him, trying to keep my tears at bay. He crooks his arm toward me, asking, "Are you ready, *mikrí prinkípissa*?" I nod again, words still escaping me, and he leads me upstairs through the amazing kitchen that has gray marble countertops, a massive matte black double oven, and light gray cupboards. It's beautiful. We head to the French sliding doors that lead to the backyard, and the ladies head in one by one, while Mila holds Sofia's hand as they stand in front of me, waiting as Etta James' "At Last" plays.

As I move forward, I see how pretty the backyard is. I also notice Ares in a little black tux in Mila's basket instead of flowers, causing me to giggle while my father shakes his head, chuckling.

"You and that fucking cat. Have you thought of names for the German shepherds yet?" I grin at him. Before getting dragged to the basement, I saw she dogs for a few minutes, and I knew instantly what I'd name them.

"Copper and Bluey." Their names fit their colors. He grins again, shaking his head, and when Christina Perry's "A Thousand Years" plays, tears fill my eyes. A few fall, and my father wipes them away before he leads me to the double doors. As we pass through, I see our families all standing and smiling at me, and as my gaze snaps to the front, I finally see *him* standing in a black tux, his eyes shining.

My Alex.

My tears start to fall again.

He planned all this for me, for us.

My father walks me toward him, and I notice Damian has a hand on Alex's shoulder while holding Maksim in the other arm, and Sergi smirks while holding baby Rora, standing next to Damian. I giggle, realizing Damian is holding Alex back. This past month, being with him again, it's like the old me has returned, and the Angel of Death has gone to sleep—well until I get an assignment from my uncle, anyway. Alex always accompanies me when I go on a mission; we're closer than ever, and once we finally talk about everything, I have no doubt we'll be unbreakable.

Alex shakes off Damian's hand, and comes down the steps and takes my hand. My father hugs him, then sits next to a very pissed-off Selene.

Oh, please, please make a scene. I feel giddy at the prospect of finally hitting her.

Alex shakes his head at me, noticing the expression on my face as I look toward Selene. It's hard to believe we used to be best friends, well, she was mine. It turns out she was using me all along.

Alex leads me to the altar, where the minister starts our ceremony. He holds both of my hands while staring into my eyes, and when the minister asks, "Is there a reason these two should not be wed? Speak now, or forever hold your peace."

I raise a brow at Alex and mouth, *"Three...two...one...."*

Selene opens her mouth. "Actually, I do!"

Alex chuckles then grabs my hands, keeping me from grabbing the pistol I have strapped to my thigh under my dress.

Spoiled sport.

I frown at him, causing him to chuckle again.

The family starts laughing. They knew she would do this; honestly, I thought Mindy would come running in. My father goes bright red while she frowns at everyone, and I giggle when I notice Damian handing cash to Sergi. Alex looks over and shakes his head at their antics. My father's angry voice brings my attention back to them.

"Selene, sit down now!"

She shakes her head. "I'm three months pregnant, and it's Alex's."

Alex's face goes red, but I squeeze his hands so he knows I know it's crap. This time it's Maria who laughs her ass off. She stands and goes over to her, grabbing her hair, and yanking it back. We all look at her in shock while Dimitri subtly tries to rearrange his pants, but not subtly enough because Damian pretends to gag, making me chuckle. I look back at Maria, and fuck does she look pissed.

My mother-in-law is badass as she growls, "Considering my son hasn't left Phoebe's side, I don't see how he would be a father to an invisible baby."

Selene screams, looking at our father for help, but he just leans back and crosses his arms, and I smirk as she continues trying to ruin our wedding.

"I *am* pregnant, and he is the father."

When I notice something on her dress, I laugh out loud.

"So you're not on your period right now, or is the blood on your ass part of the dress?" I raise my brow, then turn to Alex.

"Can I shoot her now?" I ask seriously, and he shakes his head, smirking at me, then looks at the minister and says, "Please continue."

Selene screeches, and we see Victoria dragging her out, while Maria brushes her hands together like she's dusting them off. We all laugh as I look back at Alex.

He squeezes my hands and says, "Can we marry now, Phoebe? I've waited long enough to make you my wife." I smile.

The minister continues, and when he pronounces us husband and wife, Alex yanks me to him and kisses me hard and passionately.

Finally, the minister says, "You may now kiss the bride."

Our family laughs and cheers as he picks me up and spins me around. He puts my feet back on the ground and leans his forehead against mine as tears glisten in his eyes.

"I love you, *Malen'kaya Ptitsa*."

I smile wide and say, "Not as much as I love you."

He chuckles, then picks me up bridle-style, and walks toward the tables on the other side of the yard that're decorated with pink and white roses in the center. I smile softly as he sets me down on some type of dance floor, and Ed Sheeran's "Perfect" starts to play. I wrap my arms around Alex's neck, while his go around my waist, with one hand lying just above my ass as I lean on my tiptoes, holding him close as we sway.

He leans down and murmurs the words to the song in my ear, making me tear up again, and I hold him tighter. When the song is finished, he lifts me so my mouth meets his. He kisses me with pure love as our family claps and whistles.

For the next three hours, we eat, sing, dance, and have a fun time.

A little while later, I'm talking to Avery, who came to say bye; she has class in the morning and has only four months left before she graduates and starts her residency at General. Alex comes up behind me and wraps his arms around my waist, making me turn around a little and look up, then smile wide.

He smiles down at me before looking at Avery and saying, "Thanks for coming, Av's."

She smiles and says, "Of course, I wouldn't have missed this for the world." She leans in and hugs us both at the same time. I look over her shoulder and see Sergi watching her every move, and I give him a small smile. He returns it, but it doesn't meet his eyes. I've tried to convince Avery to talk to him, but as far as she's concerned, she's done. Apparently, Mindy has been shit-stirring again. Whether it's true, I don't know, but if it is, Sergi is losing his balls.

Avery leaves without looking at Sergi, and Alex leans down, whispering in my ear, "Is my wife ready for bed?" Then he nips my ear, and my heart starts to race as wetness gathers between my legs. I smile; he's in for a big surprise.

I nod, making him growl, before he turns me around and lifts me over his shoulder, carrying me in a fireman's hold. I start laughing, and our family wolf whistles as Alex shouts, "'night, fuckers!" and slaps my ass, making them laugh along with me.

twenty-seven

Alexandr

I JOG up the stairs to our room, my gaze glancing over the pictures scattered on the walls of us and our family over the years, and I smile. This is our life and our home.

When I get to our room, I open the door and walk inside. The walls are painted half-dark gray on the bottom and cream on the top, and there's a massive king-size bed in the middle of the room. I chuck her on top of it, causing her to giggle.

I climb over her and whisper, "How pissed are you going to be if I tear your dress?" She glares at me, and I chuckle. Then, ever so gently, while looking into her eyes, I move my hand behind her back, and I start undoing the millions of fucking buttons. Thankfully, she'd already taken the outer bit of her dress off with her veil after the ceremony.

She looked fucking gorgeous when she came into view, walking down the aisle to me, and I'm so fucking glad she didn't believe Selene. We can now finally leave the past behind. She lifts her left hand, her rings shining in the moonlight, places it on my cheek, smiles softly at me, then lowers it and tugs my bowtie. She fingers the buttons on my shirt, and I'm thankful that I left my jacket and waistcoat downstairs.

When she opens the shirt and sees the tattoo of a sparrow with the letter P hanging from its beak, her eyes glisten. I lean down and kiss her softly, before I pull her dress down.

I move my lips from hers and kiss along her jaw, then down her neck, and I pull the dress past her perky tits, making my mouth water as they pop free from the material. I lean down and slowly rub my tongue around her nipple, then it into my mouth. She arches into me, moaning loudly.

After giving her other breast my avid attention, I smirk at how responsive she is and continue to kiss down her body. When I get to the scar on her chest, I gently kiss it before moving further down, her dress going with me. I roll off of her and the bed, and pull the dress completely off her, and my mouth fucking waters as my cock gets so hard it's uncomfortable. She lays on the white and gray sheets looking stunning, her tits in view, the tattoo on her shoulder standing out beautifully. She's wearing a tiny, blue thong, and heels. Fuck me, what a sight!

I lean forward and sniff her cunt through the material and groan; she smells divine. I open my mouth and suck her pussy through the material, and she moans, making me smirk. I know she's done this before, which pisses me the fuck off, but I'm going to make sure she forgets that other dick, who has ten fingers and toes that need removing.

I grip the material and rip it away from her body, tearing it, but I leave her heels on. They will feel fucking awesome digging into my ass. I grab a hold of her thighs and spread them open, displaying her for me. Her cunt glistens with need—she's fucking soaked.

"Fuck, baby, you look delicious," I say, looking into her eyes.

Her face flushes, making me smirk wider, and I dive in. I run my tongue from her ass to her clit, circling it before dipping my tongue into her cunt, then going back to her clit. I gently lick over the nub, once, twice, before I gently suck on it. Her legs start to quiver as I run my finger over her entrance, before slowly dipping inside.

Fuck, she's tight. I thrust slowly, then add another digit and curl them, before I find the magic spot that causes her back to arch as she pushes her hips against my hand. I lean forward and suck hard on her clit while I fuck her with my fingers, and she screams as wetness gushes out, and I lap up her orgasm. Once it fades and her shaking stops, I slowly pull my fingers out and stand up.

I smirk at the sedated look on her face and get undressed, freeing my cock. After removing all of my clothes, I grip my rock-hard cock tight, running my tongue along my bottom lip, still tasting her, then I bite it. She smiles at me, and I lean over her, crawling up her body. I take a nipple in my mouth, sucking it hard.

"Alex," she moans.

I kiss her neck, then whisper in her ear as I nudge the head of my cock at her opening, "You ready for me, *malen'kaya ptitsa*?"

She nods and wraps her legs around my waist, her heels digging into me, causing me to groan in pleasure as she gives me better access. I nudge forward a little, completely stunned by how fucking tight she is.

If I didn't know she had already fucked someone else, I'd say she was a fucking virgin!

I wish.

I lean down and kiss her, not wanting to ruin this moment, and I thrust forward hard. She screams, and I freeze, realizing I just ripped through a barrier. I lift my head in shock and look down at her. She has her eyes squeezed shut as a tear slides down her cheek.

I whisper, "Phoebe?" confused as fuck, and when she opens her eyes, they're glossy, love shining through.

She rasps, "How would you feel if I told you that the farthest I ever got with another guy is kissing him?"

A sob works up my throat. "You never…?"

She shakes her head. "I tried once, but I couldn't; the intended guy turned out to be a bastard, and I couldn't even get wet for him anyway. It's all yours. All of me has always been yours."

A tear slips down my cheek, and I lean my forehead against hers and say, "I love you. I'm sorry, I went in hard. Are you okay?"

She smiles, leaning up, and kisses me.

"Take me, Alex, please move. I promise I'm okay."

I nod and slowly pull back, watching her face for any discomfort, before thrusting forward. She grips me tighter and moans as she closes her eyes, but I can't have that. I grab a hold of her hair and yank her head back, making her open her eyes.

"Keep those eyes on me, sweetheart."

She tries to nod, but my grip doesn't let her. I pull out again and thrust forward, still watching for any sign of pain, and when I do this a couple of times and I see she's good, I thrust even harder, again and again, and again, until I'm going faster and faster, all while I stare into her beautiful eyes.

Her body starts to tighten around me.

"That's it, sweetheart, come for me, come on my cock. Squeeze me, baby."

I let go of her hair, keeping my other arm by her head, holding me up, and move my other hand to her clit. I press down on it and rub in tight circles. She screams, and my mouth quickly covers hers, stealing her moans as she comes hard, her body shaking as she squeezes my dick tight. I groan into her mouth as I spurt my cum into her womb, making sure it's all in there. I keep moving my hips slowly as I stop the kiss to look at her, and I can't control my emotions.

"Thank you, *Malen'kaya Ptitsa*."

She swallows and nods as tears leak down her cheeks.

She whispers, "I love you."

I lean down, kissing her again, as I slowly move in and out of her, getting hard again.

We make love all night; I don't allow her to rest. Knowing I'm the only one to have her has made me insatiable and possessive. I can't get enough of her.

The next morning, I wake up with my arms wrapped tightly around her, my chest to her back, my face in her neck, and I smile, pressing light kisses to the back of her neck, as my dick stands at attention. I move my hand down her body, and as I reach her thigh, I pick it up and slowly nudge my cock at her entrance. She sighs in her sleep, and I smile into her neck as I push forward. She moans as her hand comes up behind her and gently grabs hold of the back of my neck, holding me to her.

"Good morning, wife."

She looks back at me and has the most beautiful smile on her face.

"Good morning, husband," she whispers back, then leans up, and I lean down. Our lips meet in the middle, with my tongue tangling with hers as I move in and out of her with hard thrusts. I play with her clit as I make love to her. We do this for most of the morning, including in the shower, before we venture downstairs.

As we get to the living area, my side of the family is all there drinking coffee, and as soon as Mila sees us, she screeches loudly and runs to us. I pick her up, and she grabs Phoebe's neck, holding us tightly before I catch Damian's eyes. He smiles wide at us while he holds Rora, with Sofia under his other arm, smiling, too. I see Maksim with Sergi, while my parents look at us with proud smiles. I look down at my wife to see she's already looking at me with all the love shining in her eyes, and I melt. I lean down and kiss her gently as Mila giggles.

Fuck, I love my life.

twenty-eight

Phoebe – One Month Later

I SIGH as I sit on the sofa swing in our backyard while Copper and Bluey are running around, chasing Goosy, as Ares sleeps on the sofa next to me.

The sun is starting to set.

After my doctor's appointment this morning, I spent the rest of the day at the school, and now I'm just waiting for Alex to get home. I know he's with Damian and Sergi; they're meeting with the other Family heads about what to do with the Cartel and Romanians.

They are still kidnapping and selling children to perverts. I think I've assassinated over fifty people in the last month, and saved over fifty-six children. Alex has been with me every time, and sometimes Sergi and Damian, too. Sofia insisted he help, making him chuckle. I have not checked the app on my phone to see where Alex is. I have been getting better with my anxiety, but after my little shock this morning, I believe we now need to have the talk we have been putting off for months. Things have been perfect between us, but it's still always in my mind; he is my everything, and though we were separated those five months and I tried moving on with other men, I never could. Yet he fucked other women, several times, including with my sister.

I need to understand it so I can finally move on and leave it behind us. I still picture him and Selene together, and it's hard. This is something we have to do for our future and our family.

I hear the front door open, and I smile. I can't help it.

"*Malen'kaya ptitsa?*"

Bluey starts to bark excitedly, while Copper continues to annoy Goosy. I shake my head as Alex comes outside; he's unbuttoned the top half of his shirt, and I start to drool. Again, I can't help it. He has a body any woman would love to sleep next to. He smirks when he sees my reaction before he shows Bluey some attention. He walks over to me, and our dog goes to help Copper annoy Goosy again.

As he gets closer, I see his tattoo, and I smile. I remember seeing it for the first time on our wedding night. My heart was full of love.

He leans down and kisses me softly, before he licks the seam of my lips, and I grant him access. He holds the side of my neck as our tongues tangle. He slows the kiss, much to my disappointment, and places a few little kisses along my jaw before whispering, "I missed you, baby."

I smile at him. I've gotten better about him calling me baby, which is good because he loves using the endearment. He kisses me a few more times then goes into the house to get himself a beer. I watch him go to the kitchen, the muscles in his back moving with each step, and a conversation with Abby comes to mind.

Maybe they do back porn as well as arm porn, too? I'll have to ask her when she calls tomorrow.

When he comes out, he walks over to me, places his drink on the table next to the swing seat, picks me up, sits down, and then plants me sideways on his lap. I rest my head in the crook of his neck, my feet on the other side of the seat. He starts to swing the seat gently while he plays with my hair. I sigh in contentment. This has been our routine for over a month, and I love it.

"How's my girl doing today?" he rasps against my head, and I smile, my eyes closed, snuggled up to him.

"I'm doing okay." I feel him nod against my head where he rests his chin, and we sit like this for a little while before he talks again. He can read me like a book.

"What's on your beautiful mind, *malen'kaya ptitsa*?" he murmurs.

I stay under his chin when I announce, "I think we should talk about the past and finally let it all go." I feel him stiffen beneath me. He hoped we wouldn't have this talk, but it's needed.

"Why Phoebe? We're happy. I nearly lost you, finally married you, and we've built a life together. Why bring up memories that are going to bring back all the hurt and pain I caused?" He says it slowly. And I sigh. I move my nose into the crook of his neck and inhale deeply, smelling his musky cologne and a scent that's all him.

I whisper, "Because it's not in the past; it's still in my head. Just because I don't check the app much anymore doesn't mean it's not still on my mind every day. If we truly want to live happily together, we need to confront our past to move past it. I keep picturing you two together, and I know Selene has been trying to call you this past week. I can't let the hurt go if we just act like it didn't happen...because it did." His body vibrates against mine; obviously, he didn't realize I still have people keeping an eye on my sister and her phone.

Well, he knows now.

He stands up with me in his arms, then sits me on the seat again, and he starts to pace. It's hard to concentrate when he looks that good, but I do. I bring my knees up to my chin, where I rest it; my feet overlap on the edge of the seat.

I sigh and then whisper, "You never asked why I just left the club that day. I woke from my coma, and it was like you pushed everything that happened away, but you can't push it from my mind."

He stops pacing and looks at me with tears in his eyes, then he drops his head. It breaks my heart to bring this up, but I know it needs to be done. This is something I know I'll use against him if we argue in the future, and I don't want that, so I tell him, "If we argue in the future, what's stopping me from bringing up your mistakes to punish you? I don't want to do that; you'll resent me over it, so we need to do this, and then we can properly move on. It's more important now than ever."

He remains silent, and I swallow down my anxiety.

"I left the club that day without a thought to my safety, my mind spinning, not paying attention to my surroundings...because you just stood there," I say calmly; he needs to know. Yes, I've forgiven him, but it still hurts. I don't want to argue, I just want to put this all to bed once and for all, for our family's sake and for our love.

He looks up at me, his hands on his hips.

"I don't understand. What do you mean I just stood there? I was letting you do your thing, Phoebs."

I

shake my head. How can he be so clueless? "

Yeah, while Candy's arms were wrapped around you, and you just let her, you didn't shove her off of you, which is what you should have done."

He growls in frustration. "I was in shock that she had the balls to do it; I didn't want to hurt a woman, Phoebe. If it pissed you off so much, why didn't you fight for me? Why didn't you pull her off me? I fucking killed her as soon as you walked out! I sliced her neck!" His voice gets louder with each word, and I shake my head. How could he turn it around on me?

I speak calmly, " I was still testing you, Alex. I'm not the one who wronged you; you wronged me. You were supposed to be proving yourself to me, and you failed, epically." I take a deep breath. "Five minutes and fifty-eight seconds—that's how long you let her touch you while you did nothing. After that, I'd had enough of watching you be clueless and finally decided I couldn't be with you." A tear slips out, and I whisper, "I nearly died because you couldn't understand how to push her away from you. In that moment, all I could see was your lips on Selene's, Candy on the floor at the club sucking you off, or you fucking Mindy. I didn't fight for you because I didn't think it was worth fighting for anymore."

Tears run down his face, but I don't stop.

"For five months, you went from woman to woman, even after you realized I left—and still, knowing the reason, you still fucked other women. I couldn't even get a tingle when another guy kissed me; it felt wrong, like I was cheating on you, even though you didn't care. Even before I left, you made me fall in love with you, a man who was still happily fucking my sister. You made sure that you were my everything, even though I wasn't yours because, if I was, you would have realized that sleeping with your fiancée's sister was a bitter betrayal of what you felt for her."

Tears now run down my face. I feel like a weight has been lifted off my shoulders, and I continue, "We needed to talk about this; in the end, I still would have left you again, because these feelings would eat me alive. I don't want to resent you or throw your wrongdoings in your face. I want to be happy with you. We can't just brush this under the rug, Alex, you know we can't."

He turns away from me, making my heart jump in my chest while more tears fall from my eyes. I watch him watch the animals, breathing heavily, and hoping and praying he doesn't fall back into his old ways.

twenty-nine

Alexandr

I BREATHE HEAVILY.

I fucking hate this. I get why she wants to talk about this, but I don't want to, either. I know I messed up big time, but we've been happy. We're supposed to move on, but I guess that was naïve of me.

I turn and look at her, tears falling from her beautiful green eyes, and I sigh, hating that I've made her fucking cry *again*. I walk over to her and lean down, wiping her eyes with my thumbs as I place a gentle kiss on her lips.

I whisper, "Just give me a second baby?"

She nods.

I walk back into the house, go to the living room, and get my phone out. I find the number I want and press the call button. She answers after it rings three times.

"Alexandr? Is everything okay?"

"Mama," I rasp

She sucks in a breath. "What's wrong?"

I sit on the edge of our sofa, looking at all the photos of Phoebe and I on the mantel above the fireplace, and take a deep breath.

"She wants to talk about the past; I just don't know if I can. I really fucked up back then."

She sighs. "Sweetheart, this is probably something she really needs. Neither of you actually faced your problems; you managed to ignore the way she left you because she nearly died, and I know you wanted to make things right without bringing back the hurt and pain, but it'll only ruin you both in the long run."

I groan and drop my head, my elbows leaning on my knees.

I whisper, "What if she realizes how much I fucked up and thinks it's too unforgivable? What if she leaves me again?"

I hear my mother sniffle, then there's a shuffle, and my father's voice comes on the other end of the phone. "Son, I know how hard this is, believe me, I've been in your shoes before, but you need to talk to her. She needs this to move forward. I know it feels like you have moved past it all, but she has not. It's still in her mind. This isn't something you can sweep under the rug."

I clear my throat, keeping control of my anger, hoping I don't bite my father's head off since he's just basically admitted to cheating on my mother.

I rasp, "She knows about the phone calls I keep getting from Selene, but she thinks it's something else."

He sighs. "You need to talk to her, son. I know you didn't want to tell her, but you need to. This will only build up, and you'll lose her anyway. You can do this, I promise."

I groan again, and rasp, "Okay. Thanks, *Papa*." Then, I hang up.

I have not called him Dad in Russian in a long time.

I drop my phone on the table, notice another message, and sigh.

> Selene: please. I just want to talk to her. Father's getting me the help I need. I just want to make things right before I leave, please.

I ignore it and head back to my girl; Selene doesn't deserve shit from my woman.

When I step outside, she's sitting in the same position on the swing. She looks absolutely beautiful with her hair in a knot on her head. She's wearing black leggings and one of my shirts, too. I sigh and walk out toward her where I crouch down in front of her, wrapping my hands around her feet. I look at her, her eyes shining, full of sorrow, love, and hope, and I know that this talk *does* need to happen. She's not looking at me with disgust like she used to, she just wants to move forward.

"Okay, *malen'kaya ptitsa*, let's talk," I rasp, and she gives me a beautiful, watery smile. I stay where I am and start to rub the bottom of her feet with the heel of my hands. "Let's clear something up, first. Yes, Selene is messaging me, but not for the reasons you believe. Your father has convinced her to get help after he went to see her at her new apartment, which was a dump. She was high off her ass, and she's now going to rehab, but she's been pestering me to get to you. She wants to see you before she leaves but, I'm sorry, baby, I don't want her anywhere near you, and I've told her such once before. I ignored the rest of her calls and messages.

"I know you'll probably be pissed at me for not telling you, but we're in a good place, and my gut tells me she's going to try and stir up shit before she leaves as punishment for being happy, and I won't have it."

She nods, her eyes still holding love that shines through for me, and I smile, knowing I made the right decision where Selene is concerned, and I take a deep breath.

"There are no excuses, exceptions, or reasons for what I did. Did I believe in my mind that it was okay, so I didn't pressure you into something you weren't ready for? Yes. Did I believe that because I didn't fuck Selene in her cunt, it was okay to do what I did? Again, yes. Did I believe it was fair game to get a mistress when you left, and continue to see her when I was told the reason why you left? Yes, I did. Did I believe that because I was told you fucked someone, it made it okay to continue fucking those women? Yes, I did." Tears spill from her eyes, and it guts me. This is why I didn't want to do this, but I continued for her.

"Did I believe that I was punishing you for leaving me and planned to keep a lover even after you returned as punishment? Yes, I did."

A sob comes out of her mouth, and I let go of her feet, move from my crouching position, and kneel in front of her. I take her face in my hands, and I sigh with relief when she leans into my touch instead of shoving me away.

I whisper, "I love you. I love you so much. I have no excuses because it's all bullshit. I was arrogant, and I ignored the shit my brother went through, thinking I was invincible. I thought that once we married, it wouldn't matter, because I wouldn't sleep with anyone again. I knew what I was doing was wrong, especially who I was doing it with, but I never thought they'd have the balls to tell you because of the dirt I had on them.

"I was an idiot, a man who loved you so much but was blinded and cocky. I thought you'd never leave me, and then you did, and I broke. All I could think of was how much I would hurt you when I got you back and saw how I easy it was for me to be with other women. But I was dead inside."

She sobs again, but she's right; she needs this.

"Then Damian told me about your email, but he didn't see it until about a week before we finally found you. When I realized why you left, my guilt ate me alive, and I drowned in sorrow and pain I couldn't deal with, so I decided to bury it with Candy. I was an idiot. there's no reason or excuse for what I did, and I pay for that mistake every day. And when I found you on the sidewalk bleeding out...." I let out a shaky breath. "I instantly knew it was my fault. I knew seeing Candy wrapped around me broke you; I saw it in your eyes, that you made peace with leaving me. After everything that's happened since then, I decided to bury that day and the things that led up to me almost losing you, because I knew the guilt would eat me alive. I knew it would kill me." I swipe her tears away with my thumbs as I lean my forehead against hers. "I love you so much, and I'm so sorry for everything I've done, but know this: you are all I see, you are all I'll ever see."

She nods as a sob comes out again, and her floodgates open. I stand and lift her, then sit down, making her straddle me. She lays her head in the crook of my neck while she cries, and my eyes start to water, hating what I have done to her.

Her cries die down after a little while, and I think she's asleep until she whispers, "I'm pregnant."

My heart races, and my tears fall down my face.

Pregnant?

I place my hand on her cheek, lifting her face so I can see her, and put my other hand on her stomach.

"Pregnant?" I whisper as more tears fall from her eyes.

She nods and says, "I went for my four-week check-up on my liver and bowels today before they start seeing me bi-annually. They ran a blood test when I told them I'd been feeling sick and dizzy, and it came back positive. I'm four weeks."

I let out a little sob. Our wedding night, she fell pregnant on our wedding night. I lean forward and kiss her gently at first, then passionately, my tongue massaging hers while I grip her neck with one hand, while caressing her stomach, where our baby is nestled, with the other.

I slow down the kiss and lean my forehead against hers. I rasp, "That's why you wanted to have this conversation now?"

She nods. "I love you so much, and I love our baby, but I didn't want to go through this hormonal pregnancy taking my anger out on you. I saw how Sofia was during the end of her last pregnancy." I chuckle at that, now feeling fucking grateful she wanted to do this now; my girl's dangerous on a good day.

Chuckling, I state, "I'm hiding all sharp objects and weapons until after you give birth." She bursts out in laughter, then leans into me, placing her head back into the crook of my neck and breathing me in while I play with her hair, watching our crazy animals chase each other as Ares sleeps.

We sit like this for about half an hour, when the back gate opens. I look at my parents walking through, and I smile. I knew they'd end up popping around; they saw how bad I was when we thought she wouldn't make it. The dogs go crazy and greet them, before Goosy squawks, and the dogs chase him again, making me shake my head. The fucking bird needs to stop antagonizing the other animals. It was the goats yesterday, which I think he regretted when they head-butted him.

Phoebe lifts her head and smiles when she sees who's here.

My mother states, "We just wanted to make sure you both are okay." She has worry etched all over her face.

"We're okay, *Mama*."

I smile at Phoebe calling her mama in Russian; Sofia does, too, and my mom loves it. She sighs in relief and leans into my father, leaning her forehead against his shoulder. He looks at me with sorrow in his eyes. My mother was clearly worried about this. I feel guilty for calling her to begin with, and my father just shakes his head, understanding where my mind is going. I nod mine in understanding; I always go to them when I need to.

I look at Phoebe, and she smiles at me, making me smile back. My girl knows what my mom needs.

I clear my throat. "Hey, *Mama*?" She looks back up with tears, and I smile softly. "It looks like you've got another grandchild on the way." Her tears fall as a massive smile stretches across her lips, and then she squeals, causing us all to laugh while my father's grin is wider.

Phoebe gets off me and goes to my mom, and they hug while I get up to go to my dad. He hugs me and whispers, "Well, now it makes sense, why she wanted to do this today."

I nod and say, "Thank you, *Papa*."

My dad's eyes brim with tears, and he hugs me again before my mother comes over and grabs hold of me. While my father hugs Phoebe, I hear him say, "Thank you for giving him a chance. We love you, you know."

I feel emotional as my mother lays her head on my chest, squeezing me tight as Phoebe smiles wider at my dad, and nods. My heart feels so fucking full.

We sit for a few hours, talking, laughing, and enjoying the evening. My mother calls my brother and Sergi to spill the beans, and he, the kids, Sergi, and Sofia all come around with massive smiles. We order food, enjoy being together, and celebrate the new life we will bring into the world.

This is my family, and I smile wide.

thirty

Phoebe – Four and a Half Years Later

I SMILE as I put my veterinary certificate on my bedside table, feeling proud that I finally have my degree and that I'm now a licensed vet. I place my hand on my stomach, close my eyes, and breathe. Our whole family is downstairs to celebrate, and I just need a little breather.

It's been a difficult four years, being a full-time wife and mother, and attending veterinary school.

Who knew my husband was so jealous and possessive?

So many times he showed up to stake his claim, I still giggle at the thought. It's been nearly five years of marriage, and I'm still all he sees. I never thought it would happen; I thought he'd get bored, but he proved me wrong. He's bound by me as much as I'm bound by him now, and I couldn't imagine my life without him.

I hear footsteps and turn to see my man walk into our room. He looks at me and smiles.

"There's my graduate. Your father was wondering where you were."

I smile. My father and I are finally close again. It took a long time, but he's been amazing. Selene, however, is not in my life, much to her dismay. I know she sought out help with all her problems years ago and is attending meetings regarding her drug abuse. She wants to reconnect, but I'm not there yet. She's only just started to try to contact me by phone these past few months.

Before that, she had been calling and messaging Alex for years, which escalated when she found out we had a baby. But he knew me well, because I wasn't ready then, and I'm just not ready now. I mean, she tried to *sell* me. I know my father has been by her side since she entered rehab years ago, and his new wife is supportive, but he knows not to push me. I know Selene has a steady job and an apartment that she paid for by herself, this time in a better neighborhood than the one my father went to see her in before going to rehab, but again, I'm just not ready; a lot of water under the bridge, and all that.

Maybe one day.

I nod and walk over to him, pushing thoughts of my sister away and wrapping my arms around his waist. I lean my head on his chest and ask, "Where are the kids?"

He chuckles. "With Juan, if my mother hasn't stolen them yet."

I snort. Our oldest, Vladimir, is nearly four years old, and he's a carbon copy of his daddy. Our second oopsie baby, Nicholas, who is two and a half, was conceived not long after his big brother was born, and he is a carbon copy of me. Alex was one proud man, especially since I was on the contraceptive shot. It took a while for him to calm me down because I knew that's what the women he slept with were on, and he had to show me all the paperwork on his mistresses to prove he didn't father a child with someone else. That was the only time I brought back what he did to me. I barely ate for a week after that because of the guilt.

I promised him I wouldn't bring it back up once we had our talk, but I did, and the only reason I didn't eat for a week was because that's how long it took for him to convince me it was okay. He ended up getting his mom, Sofia, Abby, and Avery involved.

Then we have our third child, Michalis. He's one, and takes after both of us. I told Alex no more children, even though I want a little girl, but I want to get my practice up and running before anything else. I'm still hunting traffickers, much to my husband's dismay, and I can't do that while pregnant, and he can't fight me on it because, well, he's also a cold-blooded killer for the Mafia and Bratva, and is now underboss for his brother, after Sergi stepped down.

Damian and Alex fought him tooth and nail; they wanted him right where he was, but Sergi had bigger plans, even though it took him a while to accept them.

And as usual, Alex's super sperm doesn't listen to what I want. Despite the shot and condoms, he still managed to knock me up again. I'm so going to miss my leather. I look up at him when he looks down; his brows furrow when he sees my face.

"What's the matter, *malen'kaya ptitsa*?" he asks while running a finger over my brows.

I look him in the eyes and say, "Maybe this one's a girl."

His brows shoot up, and the biggest smile appears ,before he crushes his lips to mine, picking me up. I wrap my legs around his waist, my dress pushing up my body in the process, and he pushes me against the wall. His right-hand runs down my body to my underwear while his left stays on my butt, holding me up. He rips my underwear from my body, then quickly undoes his belt. He pulls his hard cock out, places it at my entrance, and thrusts it in. I moan, but he quickly covers my mouth with his so no one hears us as he fucks me hard and fast, making my insides quiver and tighten around him. He goes harder and harder, and when his thumb finds my enlarged clit, he squeezes it tight. I come, screaming into his mouth.

Alex thrusts eight more times, then moans, before filling me up. He keeps moving his hips slowly, ensuring all of his cum is in me despite already being pregnant.

He leans his head on my shoulder and says, "I fucking love you so much. Thank you, sweetheart, for giving me you and our children. Thank you for forgiving me and being my whole world."

A tear runs down my cheek, and he kisses it away, then kisses me nice and slow, making love to my mouth. I can feel him harden again, and I smile into his mouth, making him chuckle into mine. He starts to move in and out of me slowly. His hand goes back to my clit, and he starts to rub quick, tight circles on it, pressing harder in time with his thrusts.

I feel the pressure in my belly and know I'm about to come again. He thrusts faster while his mouth continues to move with mine as he pinches my clit, and I squirt all over his dick, making him come with a groan in my mouth.

He pulls out of me, still holding me up and whispers, "Fuck, I love when you squirt," making me snort. He places my feet back on the ground, ensuring I'm steady after my two orgasms, then uses my torn underwear to clean me up. He's really got to stop ruining my underwear. He sees the look on my face and smirks, making me shake my head, before he places a loving kiss on my belly, making me smile wide, my underwear forgotten.

Our fourth kid, and he's still just as excited as he was with our first. He puts his cock away, which has started to get hard again. How is that even possible?

I frown a little, making him chuckle. I can't help it. I swear each pregnancy makes me hornier than the last, fricking hormones. He kisses my forehead, and then starts to drag me, literally dragging me, down the two flights of stairs with a pep in his step, making me chuckle. He turns his head to me, smirking, then continues to drag me.

As we get to the bottom step, he pulls me to stand in front of him, and he whistles to get everyone's attention. See, fourth child and still just as excited.

They all look this way, and Sofia cheers, "About time the guest of honor showed up. You have all night to get jiggy," making me blush like a fucking tomato.

I narrow my eyes at her, and she smirks at me. Then, we both laugh outright, making everyone chuckle at our antics. Alex kisses the top of my head, and places a hand against my stomach.

"Baby number four is cooking, people. Who wants to bet it's a boy again?" I laugh at his antics while our family screams out in joy as my babies all run to me, except for Michalis. He crawls over, and I pick him up. Alex has our other two boys in his arms, smiling wide. I lean into him and look at all our family.

I feel complete and grateful that I was bound by Alex. This life was always meant to be mine, and I'd never been happier.

This is my home.

dear reader

Thank you so much for reading another one of my books! I hope you consider leaving a review to let others know what you thought. I thoroughly enjoy writing all of my books. With each one, I got more excited about the concept of their story and seeing how it flourishes through each chapter. This book shows how an Alpha Male falls deeply, with not only the heroine but also her daughter. It shows the lengths he's willing to go to to prove to her how much they mean to him, even when she's stubborn. The characters overcome their struggles as the male lead proves he'd do anything for her as he steals her heart.

about the author

C L McGinlay is a full-time mum to two boys, but also a full-time carer for her youngest, who was born with a medical condition that requires more care than the average child.

Writing is something that she's always wanted to do but never had the courage to actually do. She loves to read, and creating stories is a passion. With much self-doubt, she didn't think she could do it, but with the support and encouragement from her husband and her family, she decided to try and write to see what she can come up with. From that, the Bound series was born and, before long, more stories flowed out. When she's not taking care of her family or spending quality time with them, she's reading, then writing in the evenings. She's hopeful that people can fall in love with the characters she creates, and laugh and cry with them just like she does when she reads.

other books by charlotte

The Bound Series

Untamed Hell Fire's MC Series

Falling For Danger

Skating On Thin Ice

Printed in Great Britain
by Amazon